THE
CARRIER BAG

AND OTHER STORIES

THE
CARRIER BAG

AND OTHER STORIES

JOHN DIXON

Paradise Press

First published in Great Britain in 2012 by Paradise Press,
BM Box 5700, London WC1N 3XX

Copyright © 2013 John Dixon

British Library Cataloguing in Publication Data
A catalogue record for this book is available from the British Library

ISBN 978-1-904585-40-4

Printed and bound in the UK by Biddles, part of
the MPG Printgroup, Bodmin and King's Lynn.

Cover photograph, design and typesetting by Gill Cooper.

To the memory of the late Robert Gordon
good friend and neighbour who read and
commented on several of these stories.

Contents

Across the Corridor – and Down a Bit

Across the Corridor –
and Down a Bit

The plane landed at 3am having been delayed for several hours. I left Norman to wait for the luggage on the revolving ramp, and went to the Ladies.

I was relieved to see that the toilets were sit-downs and not squats. Perhaps, after all, Malta was more civilised, British even, than the other Mediterranean countries we'd contemplated visiting.

It was still hot at this time of night – and dusty, too. I glanced down, and there, circling inside the lavatory bowl, and never seeming to land, were a half dozen or so houseflies.

For some reason I thought of a documentary I'd seen on television. It showed the Grand Canyon, viewed from above – bleak, inhospitable and without vegetation – with two or three light aircraft circling below.

I shooshed away the flies and sat down.

What an appalling beginning to a holiday on which I'd pinned so many hopes!

'Are you alright?' asked Norman. 'You've been a long time.'

'Of course, I'm alright,' I said, irritably. 'You know me. Constitution of an ox.'

I wasn't feeling too good. The travel sickness pills were having ill effects. I was conscious of very little on the way from the airport to the hotel. I vaguely remembered being shepherded into an old bus, which Norman said looked like the sort popular in Britain after the War. I remember nothing of the journey itself, except that Norman gave a running commentary on it, saying that the headlights lit a countryside that was Biblical and red. I can remember he got excited when he saw the sea and nudged me saying, 'We must be near the hotel.' As usual he was right.

I can recall the foyer was brilliantly lit and more than I could take. The Manager greeted us heartily saying breakfast was at eight – as if we'd be up by then or feeling hungry! I couldn't face the lift. They always turn my stomach. I used the banister railing to pull myself upstairs.

'Let's have a look at both rooms,' said Norman. 'Then you can choose.'

'Either one will do me,' I said.

'O.K. then. But remember if you want anything. I'm across the corridor – and down a bit.'

'Across the corridor – and down a bit,' I repeated.

OUR FIRST FULL DAY

I feel back to my old self. I woke up my usual time and got up immediately. When I knocked on Norman's door he was still asleep. I apologised for my irritability yesterday. As ever he was all sympathy. I have never heard that man get angry – except, of course, with any pupils who were disobedient.

We compared rooms and decided not to change over. Mine had a rather pleasant view of the entrance grounds to the hotel. We chose a secluded table in the dining room and had a light breakfast.

'Well, what do you think so far?' he asked.

'You can't judge the food by breakfast. The hotel is pretty nondescript. But it'll do.'

'Pity about the parties of school children.'

I knew what he meant. There were groups from various countries and they weren't very well behaved. If Norman had been in charge it would've been a different matter.

'Shall we just potter round today? To get our bearings?'

We had discussed the holiday a lot before we came. Not this particular location, because till the last minute we weren't sure where we were going, but the idea of a holiday in general. We'd been away together often enough, but always in charge of a school party. I did the administration and the planning of the trips. Norman did all the guiding and the educational side of things. It was a good arrangement. He was the headmaster. I was the school secretary. Most of his work had become administrative. He was glad to get back to a bit of teaching.

Every summer for fourteen years we'd gone away "together" like this. Of course, some of the other teachers used to make remarks. They suspected me of having more influence on decisions than I should, even some sort of liaison. Norman must have known about this gossip, but he ignored it. He can be surprisingly tolerant.

We were both due to retire at the same time. And inevitably the subject of holidays came up. What were we going to do? I was eager to go with him. After much discussion he agreed.

'We'll have more free time together than ever before,' he said. 'We must plan things properly or we might get on each other's nerves.'

I rather doubted it but let him continue.

'We must pace it. A day relaxing, a day on a tour. Occasionally going off separately. You understand what I mean?'

I understood perfectly. I'd been living on my own for so long I wouldn't willingly give up my independence. On the other hand now Norman had retired there'd be no gossip to worry about. We'd worked together and knew each other better than we knew anyone else. If things developed so be it. I rather hoped they would. Living on a pension was not going to be easy, especially for me. Combining the two, in some way, would make a lot of sense.

He also suggested a week's holiday rather than a fortnight. I was disappointed, but it actually turned out easier booking a week at short notice. Neither of us had thought of Malta. But it was available. And would be of interest. Especially to me as my father had been there for some time during the War.

'Yes,' I said. 'Let's just potter today.'

5

The bay is quite impressive, I suppose. There are cliffs on three sides. Our hotel is on the top of the middle side. Norman says that the bay was originally a huge cave and the roof collapsed.

A special bus takes hotel residents down the cliff road to the beach. As it was our first day we decided to walk down. The footpath begins on the cliff side, which means that the view is obscured by the traffic. Also one cannot avoid the residents coming up the path and has to squeeze by. About half-way down, however, the path crosses over to the seaward side, and levels out into a pedestrian lay-by. There are a number of judiciously-placed seats, protected by a railing. In the middle is a telescope. Opposite, set back under the frowning eyebrow of the cliff and screened by shrubs and traffic signs, is a public toilet.

'Rather out of keeping,' observed Norman.

I agreed. I was afraid Norman might make a joke at the expense of my tummy trouble.

'Most of the public buildings seem to be in a mellow, restrained Baroque. But that's in Gothic. And very spikey. How odd!'

'I think it's an English Folly,' I laughed, reassured.

'Possibly. But it might prove useful if you get the belly-ache again.'

We walked on in silence.

Everyone goes to the centre of the beach where the umbrellas can be hired and the ice-cream and granita vendors have their stalls. Most of the shops are for tourists and sell familiar brand labels.

The old town, with its jetties and fishing boats, had a market for fresh fruit and fish.

'I bet we don't get any of this at the hotel!'

We were surprised by the number of local cafes and bars, some next door to each other. They were obviously not for the tourists.

'I think, if I'm not mistaken,' Norman began, 'that we have here a sociological phenomenon.'

When Norman begins like this my heart sinks. He always says 'If I'm not mistaken' when he knows he's right.

'They are rival cafes. One for the ruling political party and one for the Church.'

'We must try both.'

'But not immediately after one another,' Norman laughed.

We decided on the political one. There were Trades Union flags round the walls and black and white photos of political rallies. Most of the tables were occupied by groups of men arguing and smoking. We made our way to the counter and were rather unceremoniously waved to a table.

'I think I'd rather go outside,' I said.

It was emptier there. Norman ordered a tonic for me, and for himself the local liqueur.

'I like to enter into the spirit of the thing,' he chortled, 'if you'll excuse the pun.'

The waiter looked at us, blinked and brought the two glasses. The tables next to us, which had been empty, quickly filled with rather rough, scruffy youths. I found them somewhat unnerving, though Norman didn't seem to mind.

'Do you think they're unemployed?' I asked quietly.

'Possibly.'

They were talking in Maltese and kept looking at us. It was disconcerting not knowing what they were saying.

'Perhaps they're resentful of tourists,' I said.

'I wouldn't worry.'

'Oh, I'm not worried for myself. But it must be awful for them to produce things they can't afford and which are then exported. Perhaps they even helped produce that local liqueur and can't afford to pay for it themselves.'

'Well, I can't imagine anyone else wanting it. Frankly they're welcome to it. It's foul. Here have a sip.'

'Certainly not. Do you want to go?'

'No, not really.'

Norman can be extremely awkward at times.

We returned to the hotel for lunch. It was a drag climbing the cliff path.

'I wouldn't want to do this too often. Perhaps tomorrow we can take some food to have on the beach.'

I was hungry. My stomach had righted itself and I ate with relish, and almost immediately felt tired.

'The first day's always exhausting,' said Norman. 'All the new things to take in. How about an hour's catnap until it's cooler?'

Norman was always sympathetic. He understands me. When I'm away from home I always escape into sleep until I get my bearings.

I slept for several hours. When we met up again I apologised. He laughed –

'Why not? I waited for you and then did a bit of exploring. I got some brochures for coach tours. Here take them. You choose.' He thrust them into my hand.

It wasn't worth descending the path again before the evening meal so we sat in the lounge looking at the brochures and observing the other guests.

'Some of them live here all the time,' said Norman. 'I spoke to a few while you were asleep. Several come back every year.'

'Not the ones with those badly-behaved children, I hope.'

We discussed the children, especially the school parties. I could see that Norman was trying to take a detached view, but I knew that he wouldn't have countenanced their behaviour had he been in charge. On previous holidays, when we'd had a moment spare from looking after the children, we nattered happily on this or that current crisis. We couldn't do so now. We both realised our retirement from the school was the end of an era, not only for us but for the school itself; and that many changes we'd for so long resisted would soon be put into practice. It was demoralising to think what might be done or undone. It wasn't the subject for pleasantries. Norman had given his life to the school, sacrificed everything, family and prospects. It didn't bear thinking about.

There was an old married couple sitting at a table near us. I always enjoy trying to work out other people's characters. I consider myself a reasonably shrewd judge of personality. The woman had a most unfortunate face, rodent-like, with a jaw, chin and teeth elongated and squared-off. Norman said she had features like a coypu.

'I see what you mean.'

'And the way she chews her food. She seems to eat at the front of her mouth.'

'Yes, and as she eats she keeps her head level. She doesn't look down, does she?'

'On the look-out for danger. Protecting the family.'

'Yes, she's got a rather proprietorial look.'

'I can't see her moving quickly. Somehow she's too vacant. The rest of her is too big. If she saw danger she'd go on nibbling placidly like a cow.'

'Ah, but that makes your description of her, as the largest, slowest and longest-legged of the rodents, so very appropriate.'

'Largest?' mused Norman vaguely. 'Is the coypu larger than – say – the beaver?'

After the meal we decided on a walk.

'Let's go to the other bar.'

We walked along the cliff path and stopped at the lay-by with the telescope. The bay looked less prosaic by night, magical even. I couldn't get over the noise made by the crickets.

'There must be hundreds of them. I wish they'd show themselves.'

The second bar was quite different to the political bar. Personally I preferred it. There were fewer people, and none of the ragged youths. The walls were covered in religious paintings, statuary and candles.

'How hideous,' said Norman. 'More an expression of religion that Art.'

He then told me at length about a painting he wanted to see. It was by Caravaggio and in the cathedral in Valletta. By the time he'd finished telling me it was too late to get a bus up the cliff face. The climb took us longer than we thought.

Ominously the hotel foyer was full of activity. There was a new consignment of school children. They all looked tired. Norman made some remark – that he thought their numbers might be further reduced by sunstroke, holiday tummy and jelly-fish stings. I didn't quite catch it all as we were separated, and I found myself cornered by a new couple who promptly introduced themselves. Eddie and Rita, it might have been. They weren't very couth or prepossessing. You could see that at a glance, and if there were any doubt it was dispelled the minute they opened their mouths. I was as polite as I could be.

When I met with Norman again he said he'd met them, too.

We both wanted a good night's sleep. We decided against a coach trip next morning. There was nothing suitable till the day after. We would have an easy day on the beach.

SECOND FULL DAY

We went down to the beach early and chose a spot. I'd got quite brown yesterday simply walking round. We were just settling down to read the books we'd brought when Coypu-features and her husband appeared. They stopped and chatted. They'd been here on holiday before, to this very hotel, at this time of year. They enjoyed it so much that they wanted to come back. Anyway the husband needed a month's holiday to recuperate from a series of operations. He'd had lengths of vein removed from his legs and reinserted around his heart. There was a cross-shaped scar on his chest.

'The scars don't show so much with the suntan,' explained the wife. 'We spent the first few days at the far end of the beach. Now he feels confident enough to come down this end.'

'We've an eye on a place a bit further down,' he said.

They were obviously a devoted couple. I felt really sorry for them.

'It must be very trying for her,' I said.

'He can't feel too happy about it either.'

'Yes, but in a way her position is – well – uncertain. Vulnerable. She doesn't know what's going to happen were he to die.'

'Whereas he does?'

'No, what I mean is that she could easily overdo it and become possessive.'

'True. He must want time to himself. I only hope she lets him have it.'

We always spoke to that couple, but we didn't like to take up too much of their time.

Almost immediately they'd left, the nasty couple passed by. They spotted us just as Norman was about to take his shirt off. He is a big man with his shirt off. His chest hair is going a bit white.

'We didn't know you two were together,' the man said knowingly.

We'd been introduced to them separately last night using our different surnames. They gave us a wink. I thought for an awful moment they were going to join us.

'We're off to find a secluded spot,' the man said.

'I like to sunbathe without my top,' the woman said. 'I don't want a white line across my titties. See you around.'

We giggled and watched them disappear round the edge of the bay.

'What an appalling thought!' said Norman. 'I need something to cool down. Do you fancy a water-ice? They're nice and refreshing. Won't be long.'

'Take your time.'

'I'm afraid it's the same direction that they went. If I'm not back in ten minutes … '

' … I'll know what's happened.'

After he'd gone I must admit I slowly edged from the shelter of the beach umbrella into the sunlight. It's remarkable the difference in colour inside and outside my shoulder straps. I don't really like the line. In a way I can understand the nasty woman saying she doesn't want a white stripe across her breasts. But I don't think the sun is ever going to see my breasts. I don't think anyone is. No-one has so far – except that woman who flattens them against the cold glass of the X-ray screen.

Tonight Norman's been complaining of clawing pains in his stomach. He keeps nipping off to the loo. He said it might be a touch of what I had. He doesn't look ill but, of course, the suntan masks it.

He came down to dinner, and just ordered tonic water. The hotel food was bland and English, not even as good as school dinners. I'd never bothered much about the food when we'd been on holiday with the school children. Good food would've been wasted on them. But now I felt I deserved better.

'You're not missing much I can tell you. You were wise to stick to that tonic.'

'It looks awful. Rather you than me,' he said, forcing a laugh. 'Perhaps when we feel better we should go out to a restaurant.'

'But we've paid for the food here. We'd be paying twice.'

'Does it matter?' he asked. 'Once or twice won't break the piggy bank.'

'But it'll be wasted if your stomach's playing you up.'

'How do you know the food here isn't the cause of it?' he said.

I stopped eating and pushed the plate away.

'What sort of meals do you have at home?' I asked.

'What my Lady-Who-Does prepares for me.'

I knew of the woman who'd cleaned his house while he was at work.

'Does she do a mid-day meal now you're not working?'

'Yes, she prepares me an evening meal as well.'

I felt a slight pang at this.

'What about weekends?'

'The situation there hasn't changed. I manage myself. Nothing special. Pretty ordinary.'

'You do eat regularly? Food's important, you know, Norman. You don't think your present tummy troubles are due to years of not looking after yourself properly?'

'I'm not incapable. I don't need anyone to look after me.'

That was just the thing I didn't want to hear him say.

Personally I think this illness of his is more than just holiday tummy. It's almost certainly psychosomatic, a reaction against retirement. He's still an active man. He can't relax. One day he may be able to fill in time, do a bit of private teaching, school governorship, local politics. He's the sort of man who needs to feel fully-stretched or he feels guilty. He misses the children to organise. It's a pity there are school parties at this hotel. They're almost mocking something in him.

There's nothing I can do, except get him to drink plenty of water, bottled water. He won't take anything. He's always hated pills. Perhaps a holiday was the last thing he needed.

What it does mean is he'll be unable to go ahead with the coach visits. Fortunately we'd only booked for one tour. He insists I go.

We decided against an evening stroll and retired to our rooms. I spent much of the evening reading or just looking out the window. It's quite an interesting view, almost a view askew. The path from the entrance of the hotel grounds is at an angle to the path up to the hotel foyer. Everyone has to pass through a patch of illumination under the entrance gate. My balcony, nestling at the corner of the hotel, has a grandstand view.

You can hear the residents trailing back up the hill, and can sometimes guess who will emerge into the pool of light. Then you hear them, far less noisy now, though nearer, making their progress along the corridors.

Yes, it was nice, sitting there, looking. And knowing that Norman was just across the corridor – and down a bit.

THIRD DAY

I was glad to go on the coach. I couldn't have stayed on the beach again. I've got to be doing something all the time. Norman understands this and feels the same.

I settled down in the window seat. It was away from the sun. I put my coat and bag down on the seat Norman would have been in. I didn't want anyone sitting next to me. There was no-one I recognised from the hotel. The nice couple – Coypu-features and her husband – weren't there. I didn't expect them to be. I doubt if they go on trips. They'd probably be relaxing and sunning themselves in each other's company, as they were perfectly entitled to do. The nasty couple – I forget their names – weren't there either. They were probably at the bar or nude on the beach – or in bed!

I always set out on journeys full of expectation. I must admit though that of all forms of transport coach travel palls the most quickly – the continual stopping, not being able to move around, having to listen to the guide prattling on. But I suppose it's nice to sit there, relaxed, not actually doing anything, but still going somewhere.

We saw some interesting things. I took a few notes, even made a sketch or two, and bought several cards. I never was much good with a camera. The island is obviously very historic, dates back to pre-history. The churches are mainly nineteenth century, huge and in a mild Baroque style. The scenery is barren, parched and, as Norman said, 'Biblical.' The vegetation is mainly hedges of prickly pears. I can't say this combination did much to fire my imagination. I wondered if I'd flown hundreds of miles to somewhere rather ordinary and uninteresting.

On the way back the sun was in my eyes and I had to keep looking inside the coach – to the seat that was empty.

Back at the Hotel I asked Norman how he'd been. He shrugged and said, 'Just pottering, conserving energy.' I gave him a report of what I'd done. I exaggerated to continue the conversation, hoping I might encourage him to come on the next tour. He looked at the postcards and grunted. He must have thought I was easily satisfied. Or that I was trying to make him jealous or put pressure on him, especially when I said I wouldn't mind going back to some of the places. He had a way of dampening enthusiasm. So I toned down my report to what he obviously wanted to hear.

'The places were OK, but hardly much, hardly worth the trouble of a cramped, hot coach ride. I'm glad I went. Just to satisfy my curiosity. You didn't miss much.'

'Let's hope the one you go on tomorrow is better.'

This was his way of saying he wasn't coming tomorrow either. I had an odd feeling that he wanted his independence but resented mine.

The nasty couple – Eddie and Rita, they want us to call them – wouldn't leave us alone. They don't do this to other couples. I suspect they are not married and feel they've a right to be forward and familiar to us because we're in a similar position. I'd like to find some way of indicating that Norman and I have separate rooms.

Norman didn't seem to object to them as much as I thought he might. I'm afraid I've always tended to show my feelings. I've never been able to hide them easily. I freeze at the slightest hint of vulgarity.

A wedding ring – prominently displayed – would do wonders in warding off the wretched couple.

'See you at dinner,' they said, as they left to change.

'You won't,' said Norman, leaning over and laughing. 'I almost wish I could face dinner just to see what she wears.'

I wasn't wholly sorry Norman didn't come down for dinner. I was happy to go without as well. The food's not very good. I'm used to a big meal at mid-day. Also the heat makes you eat less.

Norman said he couldn't manage a walk. It seemed rather a waste staying in the bedroom a second evening. However there was no way I was going out by myself. I didn't like the thought of those unemployed youths. There was something threatening about them.

I'd almost finished my book and spent much time looking out the window. It was fun to see if the couples who went out together were the same as the couples who returned, or if they'd swapped partners. I tried to visualise possible groupings; where they came from, their likely backgrounds, where they'd been. I had no difficulty in telling the ones who'd get drunk, and the ones who'd end up carrying them; the ones who went ahead and the ones who trailed behind. It was amusing to watch, from a safe distance, unobserved. I don't think I could ever be like that – drunk, shouting and flirtatious.

The hotel reception never closes, of course, but the facilities stop at one o'clock. All the local transport has stopped by then. I suppose there are taxis. I expect some of the local bars stay open, the unfriendly ones probably.

I sat there waiting for the last of the guests to return. I even felt concern for the nasty couple. Inevitably they got back last. All safely back! It was like counting out the children.

I prefer to go to bed after everyone else, and think of them exhausted and asleep on their beds while I'm still awake. It would've been silly my trying to sleep in this weather. I'm a light sleeper and the noise of the doors banging and sandals flip-flopping over the marble floors above would've been unbearable.

Marble flooring is a mixed blessing. You think at first it's a luxury and cool to the bare feet, but the noise it creates for the floor below is intolerable. No, I'd rather delay trying to sleep than be wakened and not being able to drop off again.

In fact, I must have nodded off in the chair. I panicked when I woke. Where was I? What was the time? There was no light beneath the door. No light from any windows and only a reduced lighting from the foyer. Everything was quiet.

Still half asleep I looked down into the pool of light at the entrance of the hotel grounds and was surprised to see someone quickly pass through it. The odd thing was that the person was going out. I assumed it was a member of the hotel staff going home after all the clearing up had been done. The figure seemed strangely familiar. It was probably one of our regular waiters. I shrugged and went to bed.

About an hour later I woke suddenly and heard myself screaming, 'It was Norman! It was Norman!' I surprised myself and hoped I hadn't woken up anybody through the paper-thin walls.

FOURTH DAY

The next morning Norman looked refreshed. He said his tummy wasn't playing him up so much. An early night had been beneficial. He asked if I'd slept well.

'You'll laugh at this,' I said. 'I shouldn't tell you really,' and I promptly told him about my little vigil at the window and the man I'd seen going out. 'I've no idea why I should've thought it was you. You were obviously in no fit state to go anywhere. And as to waking up in the middle of the night! And shouting out! I complain enough about other people waking me up and here I am doing it myself!'

'I doubt if it was as loud as you thought.'

'I didn't wake you up?'

'I'm across the corridor.'

'And down a bit,' I added automatically. 'But even so … Oh, I don't know.'

'You're imagining things. Like you say it's just a chance association of ideas. It's better that these things come out and you talk about them.'

'As long as I didn't wake you up.'

How preposterous things seem at night! It needs the light of day to put them in perspective. He didn't seem offended that I'd suggested he'd gone out. There was no reason why he – or anyone or even I – shouldn't go out for fresh air, to think things over. But he seemed surprised that I'd been dreaming about him. Something inside me said, 'You shouldn't have mentioned that.' No-one likes to be spied on, or even thought about all the time, still less dreamt about. I'd obviously made myself look somewhat forward.

We pottered around after breakfast and used the hotel bus to get down to the beach. I was due to go on a half-day excursion starting at mid-day. Norman said he wasn't prepared to risk a tour yet. I didn't like to pressure him. I left him on the beach reading his book.

'You'll be careful of the mid-day sun, won't you?' I said solicitously. 'And do take the bus back to the hotel.'

He gave me a blank look and nodded.

The trip was delightful. I was most impressed with the old capital Mdina. It was quiet, historic and well-preserved. I bought a lot of postcards. When I returned in the evening I showed them to Norman.

'Now that looks splendid,' he enthused.

'Splendid it certainly was. I wouldn't mind going there again.'

In the evening we set out to find a restaurant. Norman was determined to go. I thought his tummy might still be unsettled.

He said it probably was and that he'd pay for the meal doubly but that he was so bored he had to do something different. I could understand that. He's certainly in better spirits than he's been for some time.

We were leaving just as everyone was coming down for dinner, clomping on the marble floors. Some, of course, seemed not to have left the dining area all day, and were sitting around or propping up the bar.

The awful couple were there. Eddie had collared the Manager, who'd made an appearance to check all was going well.

'It's got everythin', 'asn't it?' slurred Eddie. 'Lotta British. No lingo problems. You've got the sun, the beach, the pool, if you wannit. Places to see. Or you can just stay in quietly for a sherbet. Bar's open all the time. Or play one er the games. And when I say one er the games you know what I include there, doncha? You got the lot, 'aven't cher? Can't go wrong. Well, good luck to you, I say. And as for the food. It's ace. Tip-top.'

The Manager took the opportunity to point out that the food was indeed ready, and beckoned them to the tables.

'Doncha worry. We'll be coming back nex cheer. With friends, eh, Rita, gal?'

Norman glanced at me as they passed by.

'I expect the Manager would've preferred praise from almost anyone else!'

'True.'

'But give it time. People like that will soon find something to moan about. They're all over you at first, then they don't want to know.'

We went to a small restaurant at the far end of the resort. I say far end, in fact, it was the old village from which the resort had grown. We were stared at a lot and had to push past groups of men leaning by the entrance. Inside was empty. We were unsure where to sit. We didn't want to be lost to view.

'Here I suppose.'

We looked at the menu.

'I think I'd like the swordfish,' Norman began pompously.

'Is fish advisable?'

'Sword-fish is alright. It comes in steaks and is fairly solid, like tuna.'

'Really?'

'You're worrying about me too much. I wish you wouldn't. It's shellfish you must avoid.'

The waiter came to take the order. He welcomed us effusively.

'Can you tell me what this is please?' asked Norman, pointing to an item on the menu.

The waiter did not even bother to look.

'It's not available, sir. We have mixed fish. That's all. Fresh today. You can have them grilled or fried.'

'That's all?'

'There may be some fish soup left over from yesterday.'

'Soup would be ideal for your stomach, Norman.'

He flashed his eyes at me. 'Would it?'

'Well, it's very nourishing.'

He turned to the waiter. 'There's no sword-fish?'

'Not at present, sir. There will be. But not today.'

'Then it will have to be the mixed fish, won't it?' said Norman looking at me.

'Haven't you got anything else – ready prepared?' I asked.

The waiter shrugged. 'What's the point of cooking till the customers arrive? They may not want what we cooked.'

'But I'm hungry,' I insisted. 'I want something quickly.'

'Nothing will take long, Madame, and a fresh meal will satisfy you more.'

I must have looked unconvinced.

'Madame will come to the kitchen with me. And choose. You will see.'

We went to the kitchen and I must admit I was quite impressed. All the fish had been laid out in readiness and looked very fresh.

'I can recommend this variety,' said the waiter, pointing. 'It's a meal in itself. Or have a selection. Please yourself.'

'You don't keep any fish – live in tanks?' I asked significantly.

The waiter gave me a long look and pointed out the back door – towards the sea.

'There is our fish tank,' he laughed. And Norman joined in.

'But before you sit down again,' the waiter said, 'why not move to another table?' He pointed to one in the corner. 'You will be less disturbed there.'

I don't know what relationship he was assuming existed between Norman and myself. I expected Norman to object. But he thanked the waiter and we moved to the corner seat. We had a good view of the entrance one way and out into the garden and landing stage the other. The disadvantage was that it was cramped and by being in a corner we had to sit at right angles to each other. Our legs kept touching under the table. Norman didn't seem to mind. I suppose I didn't either.

The waiter took our order to the bar and the whole area came to life. The men we had taken for loafers were galvanised into action. Three of them went into the kitchen, another laid the table and one brought our drinks.

'They're more organised than we give them credit for. Not having a menu is a good sign. You get something fresh.'

'So you said before,' I remarked, irritably.

Norman does try to be right all the time. I think I ought to have some say, especially in matters of food.

'But you don't know,' I added sharply, 'what the choice is going to be.'

'That's rather nice, isn't it?' he said, sweetly. 'Or I think so, anyway. And we did choose from the actual ingredients.'

'Possibly,' I said grudgingly.

'They do things differently here, and at a different pace.'

'Oh, do they?' I said.

He could see I was annoyed. He looked at me and smiled.

'You'll feel better when you've had something to eat. You'll mellow with the first whiff of cooking.'

'Will I?'

He nodded without looking at me.

21

Fortunately the food arrived quickly. I have to admit the portions were generous, with side salad and bread. It was simple but tasty. We tried to analyse the contents.

'The fishes have been transformed. I can't make out which was which. It's delicious – whatever it is.'

'Better than the hotel.'

'I wonder what they had tonight?'

'Who cares?'

The bill was a pleasant surprise, too. It was so reasonable.

'We should've got 'Bed and Breakfast' and come here to eat.'

'I feel guilty though,' I said. 'They can't make much profit.'

'Perhaps that's not their aim.'

'No, but some of the staff here would be under employment age back in England. They'd still be at school. They'd be in bed by now. Doesn't that worry you?'

Norman looked vacant and non-committal. 'Perhaps they don't see it like that,' he replied. 'They stay up later in warmer climates.'

'I suppose so. But it is true – isn't it? – that tourists are often resented by the locals. Look at those groups of unemployed men who glowered at us in the first café we went to.'

'I can't answer for them,' shrugged Norman. 'But everyone in here has made us feel at home.'

We decided to go back there the next day.

'Let's keep this place to ourselves, shall we?' said Norman.

I agreed readily.

Several guests at the hotel asked us why we'd missed dinner. Were we still ill? We made up little stories. It was fun. We took turns to lie. 'We didn't fancy it. We had a large lunch. We went to an earlier sitting. We went to another table.'

'What if that awful Eddie and Rita ask?' I said.

'We'll say we had it brought to our rooms,' laughed Norman.

In fact, when they inevitably did ask Norman answered –

'We have several friends and relatives in Malta.'

I laughed. Norman was obviously getting back to his old self.

He mentioned he wanted to round off the holiday with a visit to the capital, Valletta. It doesn't need booking as there is a regular bus service. For tomorrow I have booked two seats on a grand tour of the island. It includes the other island, Gozo, but excludes Valletta. It covers lots I've already seen before, but also a few new places. I'm not keen on going especially as it's a full day. I hope that by the morning Norman might feel up to it.

FIFTH DAY

I didn't think I was going to spend all the holiday alone – on a coach. This time the coach was full. I managed to sell off the spare ticket. Unfortunately in my eagerness I sold the window seat and had to sit by the gangway. I couldn't very well ask the woman to change over. She seemed the type who'd engage in conversation once you started. I wasn't really in the mood so I kept quiet and let it pass. It didn't really matter as I'd seen most of the scenery anyway. But it did tend to make my mind wander – or rather concentrate on things I was trying to forget.

I don't know what I expected from this holiday. I assumed Norman might mellow because he was alone with me. I've only ever known him through his work. Only forty hours a week. What about the other – how many? – hundred and twenty eight? God, as many as that!

I suppose it was too much expecting him to appreciate me on another level. But if anyone – his silly cleaning lady apart – should've got to know him in a different context then it was me. I worked closer with him than any of the teachers. And it is I – I still marvel at the fact – who am on holiday with him.

I hate to be thought of as pushy or heavy. Familiarity and forwardness are deadly. They can only lead to a rebuff.

How does that vulgar couple succeed so effortlessly?

23

Oh God, is there anything more depressing than looking at peasants scratching a living amid the ruins of a former civilisation?

When I got back to the hotel I found a note from Norman saying he'd be at the restaurant. I hurried down there, half exhausted. He wasn't there and didn't turn up for twenty minutes.

I didn't say anything and had little to report about my trip. He seemed eager to hear the details, though. I showed him a few post cards. He said Sliema looked like any other holiday town. And of the other island, Gozo, he said –

'It's much the same, isn't it? Only smaller.'

'I'm sure that's a very good description,' I replied in a flat voice. He was excited about something.

'Aren't you going to ask me what I did today?'

'I assumed you just conserved your energy. And pottered about. As usual.'

'Not a bit of it. I went to Mdina.'

I was taken aback. 'I see.'

'I know you wanted to go there again but it wouldn't have fitted in. There's no other way to get there – save the local bus, which takes ages. And we're committed to Valletta tomorrow. I looked it all up. It was today or never. It only took half a day.'

'I see.'

'I must thank you for encouraging me to go there. It was – as you said – rather splendid. It got me out of myself. I'm sorry I've been such a bore this holiday.'

I paused . 'It's not your fault. I'm glad to hear you're getting better. Your tummy? It was OK?'

'A couple of near disasters. But it's improving. It'll be better by tomorrow.'

'You're sure you want to go to Valletta?'

'I can't miss the new capital, now I've seen the old one. Anyway I wouldn't want you to go alone. I don't mind you going on organised coach trips to small places but going on a bus to a city is another matter. It's a big town, you know. And I expect it has its seedy side – markets – and quarters – and things.'

He seemed to have regained his enthusiasm for lecturing. I felt moderately flattered by his concern. It was good to think that at long last we'd be going somewhere together.

'That's kind of you,' I said.

'Well, I know you specifically want to go there.'

I'd told him my father had been there in the War.

'If you're sure you're feeling up to it?'

'I'll be alright,' he said. 'There are a few things I want to see, too. The harbour. A couple of buildings. And, above all, a picture.'

LAST FULL DAY

We set off together straight after breakfast. We were both glad to get out of the hotel. The bus was old and crowded and we had to sit apart.

'It was worse than the one we had from the airport.'

'I was thinking that, too.'

'Well, I suppose we'll be on it again tomorrow, won't we?'

'It's gone quickly, hasn't it?'

'Let's make the most of today.'

We walked from the bus station through the city arch to the fortified town. It was far busier than I'd expected. The harbour was undoubtedly impressive. We looked at the ships through a telescope. I always thought of the Navy in terms of barracks, not very close to any amenities, rather secluded, with an occasional regatta or visit of a foreign ship. Nothing where the life of the port and the town were so closely mingled.

I was glad to be with Norman. The narrow alleys between the tall tenement blocks were off-putting. Washing was stretched from side to side. A drip of water felt like a cold blade on the neck. In one street it wasn't just washing that was hanging out the windows – but women!

'Do you think it was like this during the War?' I asked disillusioned.

'Worse probably. There are similar quarters in most parts – especially in the Med. Your father must have had a fine old time.'

My father always used to say Med. for Mediterranean. And Gib. for Gibraltar. Whether he'd had a fine old time or not when he was in Malta I really wouldn't know.

We returned to the town centre, looked at a few civic buildings, and then retired into the quiet and cool of the Cathedral. I have always been quite happy to put a veil over my head in church. It is a little role I fit into willingly.

Norman resumed his tourist guide approach and started pointing things out. He reached a crescendo when he came to the picture he so wanted to see. It was of the beheading of St. John the Baptist. It didn't do much for me. The figures were oddly illuminated and all huddled on one side. It was needlessly brutal, too. I felt so sorry for poor St. John. He was not represented at all like a noble figure, but reduced to a mass on the floor. The executioner, who was a rough, scruffy-looking man, was given much more prominence.

'The moment before the drama,' Norman began. 'Not the drama itself. How it anticipates! Salome holding the dish in readiness. The executioner's left arm holding the Baptist down by the head. His other arm behind his back and bearing the knife. That arm will straighten, arc round and plunge down and do its work. St. John's in for a surprise, isn't he?'

'Norman. You're getting quite bloodthirsty,' I said indignantly.

'That's the point,' he replied.

I shrugged and said, 'I suppose artists do have to paint Biblical scenes, but couldn't they do it more tastefully? And if executions must happen then surely in an organised kingdom they could be carried out properly by neatly-uniformed soldiers.'

Norman spluttered. 'I'm sorry you didn't like it. Especially as it's the only bloody thing in Malta worth seeing.'

'Oh, really.'

This was too much. Valletta was the only place he so wanted to see, the only time he went anywhere with me. And now …

'I'm going,' I said. 'Don't feel obliged to come if you want to go on looking at it.'

'Have a look round the Cathedral,' he said. 'Don't go outside, will you?'

I had that feeling again that he despised my opinions but worried about my welfare.

Things calmed down a bit outside. We had a coffee in a charming little square. I bought a few presents for friends. But I was glad we had to sit apart on the bus going back.

As it was our last evening we decided to brave the food and have dinner at the hotel. That would give us more time for packing. There were many new guests in the dining room and the tables had been moved around. I couldn't see Coypu-features anywhere. Possibly she'd left, or her husband had fallen ill. I couldn't very well ask about her as I didn't know her real name. And most of the staff were new and wouldn't have known.

We spent far too long on the packing. We could've left it to the morning. But once completed we felt free to enjoy ourselves. We'd seen all the places we were ever going to see. An early night seemed wrong. We went on a walk to recap. We descended the cliff road and looked over the sea. It was very calm and reflected the moon. The crickets were even noisier than usual. I still hadn't seen one.

That wasn't the only thing I'd missed out on. I'd made little progress with Norman. Perhaps another time, another holiday. Perhaps even tonight.

We mulled over the holiday. All the usual little phrases – "Not quite what we'd hoped. Reluctant to go now the time has come. Hasn't it gone quickly? Pity about your stomach. And yours. Wouldn't want to come here again. A week's ample. More than.

Some people might want more. Depends what you're looking for. Takes all sorts."

We had reached the half-way stage and walked over to the seats around the telescope. One of the rough-looking locals moved off as we approached.

'I suppose by the law of averages some holidays must be less satisfactory than others. When one goes regularly, that is.'

Norman only said, 'Yes.'

'And one does need a regular holiday.'

He said nothing.

'The thing these days is that you have to book them so early – unless you are prepared to accept a cancellation – which, as we found, is a risk. You might end up somewhere better if you booked way ahead.' I paused, then continued. 'You almost have to start thinking about the next holiday before you've finished the one you're on.'

I couldn't get bolder and more forward than that.

'I shouldn't have eaten all that hotel food,' he said suddenly. 'It's already beginning to … you'll excuse me if I pop over …' He pointed across the road.

'No, of course.'

I'd forgotten about the little Gothic loo.

I waited by the seats, and to take my mind off things I tried the telescope. It was very old and looked like a left-over from the War. Perhaps this little enclave in the cliff was actually man-made and had served as a look-out post.

I was rather surprised to find that the telescope was facing the wrong way. It was pointing towards the toilet.

I tried to move it round a hundred and eighty degrees but it would only go so far before slowly arcing back. I tried several times but it seemed magnetised. It creaked almost pleadingly the further I pulled it back, and then sprung softly and easily as if returning to its natural position.

'How unfortunate! I wonder if I should report it to the Works Department.'

At that moment I heard the vulgar couple coming up the hill. Oh, God, I thought. What does one say to them? I do wish Norman would hurry up.

'Hello, there,' I said. 'How are you?' I expected a long and involved reply, but they seemed to have something pressing on their minds.

'Can't stop,' said the woman. 'Eddie's got the runs.'

'Yeah, I got the back-yard trots.'

'Oh, I am sorry to hear that,' I said, and added rather wickedly, 'Not something you ate at the hotel, I hope?'

'We don't eat anywhere else,' he said pointedly. 'So it must be. I'm gonna sort that Manager out.'

'Norman's been suffering as well and we rarely eat at the hotel. I wouldn't blame the Manager.'

'Don't wanna know. Can't stop. Or I'll never make it.'

'Actually,' I said helpfully, 'there's a loo right behind you.' I must admit I was tempted not to tell him in the hopes the wretched man suffered the more. 'It doesn't look like one, but I assure you it is.'

'That's no good,' he snapped. 'That's just a stand up one. It's got no cubicles.'

No cubicles! No cubicles! I felt my legs give way beneath me. No cubicles! No cubicles! And Norman's been gone for a quarter of an hour!

I clutched at the telescope for support. I put my whole weight on it and pushed and pushed and pushed to make it point out to sea. But it just arced back.

Realising now what Norman is has taught me a lot about myself. I have always got on better with men who were 'safe' in one way

29

or another – older, happily married, unattainable. I met them all through work, of course – respectable office-holding men, often in uniforms. Absorbed in their work and never coarse. I suppose I assumed they had no thoughts in that direction, let alone did anything.

I can't blame Norman for deceiving me. I was naïve, almost a willing victim. Possibly he thought I knew, but was too tactful to say anything. That's probably the best way to leave it. He still doesn't know that I know.

There's no reason for me to tell him. Nothing would be gained by that.

The Carrier Bag

The Carrier Bag

It was the carrier bag that did it. We all noticed that first. The sun was in our eyes but we never failed to recognise the bag, and then the distinctive figure of its owner. We laughed every time he went by. He had to move towards the edge of the pavement to get past the chairs that had been set outside the wine bar – and, of course, because of Nigel's legs. Nigel always sat as far as possible from the shop front so he could lollop on the white metal garden chairs and stretch out his amazingly long legs – which he stretched out even more when he saw the man coming. We giggled, snorted into our glasses, raised a toast and blew a defiant puff of cigarette smoke if he dared to look our way.

'Isn't he just too awful?' said Amanda, patting Clive on the knee – which was bare. He never changed back after squash.

'God, I hope I don't end up like him.'

'Why should you? You'll have financial security long before you're his age.'

'It's the carrier bag that does it. It's the finishing touch.'

'Yes, it's so right, isn't it?'

'And it's the same one every day.'

'I'm surprised it's lasted so long. You'd think he could get another one.'

'It would still be – just a carrier bag,' sneered Amanda.

'Some bags can be very nice,' replied Cindy.

'Yes,' joined in Rose. 'You can get lovely ones now. Some of them are reinforced at the top, like a plastic coat hanger. They keep their shape, and last ages. And even the paper ones are strong, and are actually better for reproducing flower patterns.'

'Some of the William Morris ones are adorable. Not a bit like his.'

'I saw a lovely one the other day. I fell in love with it at once. I just knew I had to have it.'

We looked at the bag. It was always half empty. The base was stretched taut with the contents but the top was gathered and wrinkled.

'It looks,' said Ambrose, leaning down to finger his leather brief-case, 'it looks like a scrotum – held independent of the body.'

We all laughed, and even Angela, who was a bit of a prude, had to smile.

'I wonder what he's got in it?' said Cindy, puffing at her cigarette.

'I told you. His gourds.'

'The start of a lifetime's collection of rubbish,' said Nigel. 'I can imagine him in a few year's time – perhaps not as long as that – with an old pram.'

'Or a basket on wheels,' said Charles, who did not want to be left out the conversation.

'No, a supermarket trolley,' said Rose, going one better.

'Yes, definitely a supermarket trolley,' we all agreed.

'Not filled with goodies, but old rubbish.'

'But what's in the bag now,' persisted Cindy.

'His bag wash, I expect. He probably doesn't have a washing machine of his own.'

'Or indeed, anything of his own. '

'I bet he goes down to the public launderette.'

'Oh, definitely a frequenter of public things.'

'Libraries, lavatories, washhouses and baths.'

'And bars.'

'Yes, he probably went into the public bar, couldn't reach the public lavatory in time, and now he's going to the public launderette.'

34

We laughed.

'Fancy walking along the road with smelly clothes!'

'Smelly smalls,' said Cindy who liked little rhymes.

Angela coughed on the cigarette smoke. Now, she really was good with words and rather disapproved of Cindy's little rhymes. Angela could make a word so pointed just by leaving off the usual prefix. She often left the un off the word couth to give it a condemnatory twist. "He's hardly couth, is he? Or kempt? Or ruly?" And she often reversed the normal order of words. Anyone else would have said 'He's a dirty old man', but she said tartly –

'He's an old, dirty man.'

That seemed to finish the conversation.

Cindy asked vaguely –

'I wonder what the lettering on it says.'

'Some motto or commercial logo, I suppose,' replied Clive out of politeness.

'Not a sports logo, for sure,' said Amanda, patting Clive's knee.

Then we got to talking seriously, shielding our eyes from the sun, screwing them up as if we were in deep thought. Charles lamented he had never learnt Greek at school.

'It's marked me down.'

'Nonsense,' said Ambrose. 'It's not of the slightest importance.'

'It's easy to say that. You can speak it,' snapped Charles.

'No, he's right. I did it a bit, and I've never used it. But Charles, you're doing so well.'

'That's the important thing. Even University isn't really necessary nowadays.'

'That's true enough. None of my education prepared me for the job I do.'

'I regret I never went though,' said Clive, sadly.

'Didn't you, then?' asked Angela.

'Some of my colleagues did,' said Nigel. 'They say it was very good for contacts.'

'Well, my boss didn't. And look how well he's done. He knows everyone worth knowing. '

'Did you go to university, Angela?'

'Yes, I did – actually.'

Next day we analysed his clothes.

'The grey-brown is just typical, isn't it?'

'Like a manilla envelope. Or a bill from a utility.'

'Why do people use those envelopes when there are so many coloured ones around,' asked Rose.

'I adore Paperchase.'

'It's a horrible colour. It's like camouflage.'

'Without the distinction of khaki,' said Nigel, who had once been in a regiment.

'Oh, yes. That's quite different,' said Angela. 'It suits him though. You have to admit. He has a wonderful dress sense – in that his clothes match his personality.'

Then we talked about clothes.

'They're SO important, aren't they?' said Rose. 'They are such an indicator of character.'

'And beliefs.'

'So what can you make of his baggy trousers?'

'They CAN be effective. You only have to think of Oxford bags.'

'But not on HIM!'

'And those frayed turn-ups and worn elbows!'

'He needs an elbow patch,' said Cindy.

'He needs a lot of patching altogether. And stitching up,' added Angela for good measure.

'You look better than that,' said Amanda to Clive, 'just off the rugby field.'

'I say,' suggested Charles, 'can't we arrange for one of those parties where everyone dresses up in rags? They're such fun.'

'You mean a Down-and-Out party?'

'And you look all ruff and common-like, don' cher?'

This set Charles off doing his imitations of thickie workers.

'Cor. Yer'd unnerstan' why I'm wearing old cloves if yer'd worked as 'ard as I 'ave.'

'I say. That's awfully good.'

'Don't encourage him. He can go on like that for hours.'

'Well, shall we have one of those parties, then?'

'Yes, let's.'

'Not 'arf.'

'What shall I go as?' asked Clive.

'You'd look wonderful in anything,' said Amanda.

'I'm going to have a carrier bag,' said Cindy. 'What shall I have written on it?'

'Oxfam or Age Concern?' snorted Angela, who hated the poor and the elderly, and wasn't too keen on Cindy either.

'I don't know,' mused Cindy, lighting another cigarette. 'What do you think HE'S got on his bag? I want whatever he's got on it.'

It was a lovely evening outside the wine bar. The sun shone in our eyes, making a blind spot ahead. We loved these al fresco drinking sessions. Nigel ordered another bottle and held up a glass to the sun and said, 'To Tuscany and Chianti.'

'Real nice droppa plonk you got there, mate, innit?' imitated Charles.

'You mustn't mock. These things are important.'

'No, that's not funny. Anyway you know you can tell a good wine as well as any of us.'

'I wish my name wasn't Cindy.'

'And what would you prefer?' asked Angela coldly.

'Florence.'

'Oh,' said Angela, taken aback.

We talked of holidays, and of places we regretted not having been to. Ambrose who understood Greek and worked very hard regretted not having been to Sparta, 'though there's not supposed to be much left,' he added.

We timed each evening by the man's arrival. Each time he passed

Nigel slouched down in the chair, sticking his legs out even further.

'He'll have to walk in the gutter soon.'

'What if he stepped on your feet, Nigel?'

'I'd raise my legs. Hard'

'He probably wouldn't feel a thing.'

'I told you he keeps them in his carrier bag,' said Ambrose.

'He probably hasn't got two pennies to rub together,' said Charles, nudging Nigel. He pronounced pennies like peenies. We all knew what he really meant.

'Oh, really,' scowled Angela.

'Well, there is a correlation between poverty and impotence, you know. And vice versa.'

'Do you think there's one between a straight back and an erection?'

We all laughed again.

'Just look at him, lolloping along. As if he's crawled out the woodwork.'

'A good kick would do him good.'

'I could trip him up with my umbrella,' said Cindy. She carried an umbrella in all weathers. It doubled up as a sun-shade. It had a handle carved like a cartoon dog. Cindy loved animal stories and called the umbrella Bosun.

'Better not,' said Clive tactfully.

'Anyone his age should have his own transport by now,' said Angela cuttingly.

'True,' agreed Nigel, turning to her. 'You know – Italy is so wonderful.' He poured her another glass. 'And so musical. You would love it.' He turned to the others. 'Angela's very musical, you know.'

'Are you?' the rest of us gasped.

'I love going to galas,' she said.

'Do you play an instrument?'

'I'd love to. And I think I'd be very good at it. But I haven't had the time. I buy my ticket and pay others to play for me. I'm on several mailing lists.'

'Do you read music? It looks all Greek to me.'

'I don't actually read it. I don't think that's really necessary. I can tell a good performance from a bad one. Or if anyone's off key. I think – in fact, I'm pretty sure – I've got perfect pitch.'

'Really?'

'And have you been to many galas recently?'

'There's one next week. It's an all Richard Strauss concert.'

'I love waltzes,' said Cindy.

Then one evening, to our great delight, the man with the carrier bag stopped just before he got to us. He knelt down.

'He's kneeling to us.'

'Isn't that nice? At last he's recognised our true worth.'

'Actually, he's going to do up his shoe laces,' said Cindy.

'You don't say,' snapped Angela irritably.

'Not laces, Cindy,' corrected Clive. 'String.'

'Now, Nigel, don't be tempted with your feet.'

'What about me with my umbrella?' asked Cindy.

As the man knelt there, vulnerable as never before, he let go of the carrier bag. It flopped down and seemed to unwrinkle. The lettering was just visible.

But the sun was in our eyes. It was the blind spot again.

The man stood up and walked off quite jauntily.

'Did you see what it said?'

'It was quite clear,' said Angela. 'It was something in Greek.'

'No, it wasn't,' said Charles offended. 'How could it be? With him? You're just saying that to annoy me.'

'How would you know if it was or not?' said Ambrose. 'You don't know the language.'

'I don't think it was Greek.'

'I think it might have been,' said Rose. 'I'm pretty sure it said Sparta.'

'That's more like it,' laughed Charles. 'If you knew it so well, Ambrose, you'd have recognised it at once, surely? Especially as you've always wanted to go there.'

'There was definitely some writing,' said Cindy emphatically. 'It might have been Greek for all I know. It might have been Sparta. But there was also a kind of town crest.'

'Yes, that's right. I saw that, too,' said Ambrose. 'But I don't think it was a town crest. It was a university crest.'

'HIM! Go to . . . Now you're getting at ME,' shouted Clive.

'I'm almost positive it was. With a motto underneath.'

'That's not what I saw,' said Nigel. 'I think the crest was actually a group of musical instruments arranged together. It was definitely music underneath. Notes. Or the words of a song. Or the name of a shop selling sheet music.'

'I don't see how it could have been. With him!' snapped Angela.

'But surely you must have recognised it,' persisted Nigel.

'Are you doubting me, Nigel? Are you comparing me to him? I expected . . .'

'And what did you see, Amanda?' interrupted Rose, trying to calm things down.

'I didn't notice. I was looking …'

'… at Clive,' the rest of us groaned.

She withdrew her hand at once from Clive's knee. Nigel drew in his legs and sat bold upright. Cindy drew heavily on her cigarette, stubbed it out and a moment later blew a vast puff of smoke into Angela's face.

None of us refilled our glasses. The sun went in.

Little Gems
A monologue

Little Gems
A monologue

Brrr! Don't realise the cold till you get back indoors! All done now. Put it off too long. If I'd left them any longer – stored them over that wire rack – they'd've shrivelled up – or been nibbled by the squirrels. As it is I'll be lucky if half of them come up. Though to be fair, bulbs usually do what they're told. More than can be said for … At any rate they're in now. And before the weather changes. Brrr!

I can feel in my bones it's going to be a long hard winter. The squirrels haven't been round, and they never fully hibernate. I'm going to though. Lock myself in, and shut down. It'll be my first winter and Christmas alone. I'll have time to get on with what I want.

Currently I'm writing a biography of my three daughters. It's my way of bringing them together – if only on paper. Of course, I keep their photos on the desk.

This is my third daughter, the youngest, Amber. Incidentally, all my daughters – not my doing – are named after precious stones. Amber was last to leave home. I regretted her going most. Took her to the University interview. Nice campus, greensward edged with bedding plants, with signposts to the different departments. Months later I helped her settle in the Hall of Residence. Nice little rooms, well-lit, work surfaces under the windows, beds along the interior walls. She had to share, of course, with another girl. I never met her – well, not till much later. That's her, there. Thought of cutting her out the photo, but …

This is my second daughter, Pearl. Hardly a year between them – but very different. Pearl tried to be fun-loving, but she found her niche as a City workaholic. She became terribly conventional – but still my problem daughter. That's her favourite photo. I took it. She thought it one of the best things – one of the few good things – I ever did. It was her moment of glory. She's pointing up to … well, it takes some explaining.

And this is my first daughter, Ruby. I don't want to dwell on her too much. I couldn't even if I wanted. She's not exactly mine. A step-daughter, taken on just after birth. I don't think she regarded herself as anyone's daughter really – and once she'd had her own, she was in her element, lost to all other ties. There she is, hiding, behind the babies. We were there just to admire them – and her for having them – not to touch them. I could've enjoyed grandchildren – occasional childish company without full responsibility. Amber always liked children. Pearl, less so.

Anyway, the grandchildren – it wasn't their fault – didn't bring us together. Not at Christmas, not birthdays, theirs or ours. Certainly not mine. So, I can only bring them together on paper.

Which may be just as well. They didn't always get on. There were all sorts of alliances, fallings-out, re-alignments with the former enemy. Once they'd all left home – Pearl to the City, Ruby to Nursing College and Amber to University – a tacit routine was established. One or other of them came down every other weekend. This gave me time to myself. Time to prepare for the visit. Time to get over it. I couldn't have faced them all on at once. They might've united against me. One at a time I could cope with.

Then Pearl started bringing down male friends. I'm not good with strangers in the house. And almost all her men were very strange. Quite peculiar. Apalling, in fact. They looked and thought alike. The first was worst.

'I'm bringing someone down. Just for the day. Don't bother with food. We'll give you a treat.'

That was ominous in itself. The moment the boyfriend arrived he put his foot in it.

'How lovely to get back to country living.'

Well, this is a nice house, I grant you. Too big for my needs. But between the front gate, where he'd parked his flash car, and my front door there's a copper beech hedge, a laburnum and a magnolia. Well, if that doesn't spell suburbia, I don't know what does. I assumed he'd lived in town all his life.

'Do you know what we saw on the way down? A fox. Mangy looking thing, it was. Heading for town, for the dustbins. Easy option. Cowards – won't face a fair fight with the hounds.'

'Really?'

'Pearl said you had squirrels in the garden. Want me to borrow a shot gun?'

'No, I don't!'

Pearl hastily intervened. 'Where do you want to go for lunch?'

We ended up in an Indian Restaurant – of his choice. Couldn't complain. Extensive menu. I dreaded he'd try and prove himself by eating the strongest curry, and then throw up once he hit fresh air, or even worse, splatter the back of my lavatory bowl.

'I want what you're having,' Pearl said to him. She turned to me. 'He'll choose for you. He knows about these things.'

Did he? Come the ordering, and he mixed up poppadums and Bombay duck, and asked for Bombay drums and poppaducks. I thought at first he was just plain stupid. Then he acted out his mistake and repeated Bombay drum and started beating a tattoo on the table. Then Poppaducks! Poppaducks! Pop! Pop! And imitated shooting a duck. Pearl fell about quacking. I wanted to apologise to the waiter.

'And for the main course I'll have the hottest. Chicken Vindaloo.' This became 'Chicken Vinda–whOOps! I've gotta go to the Chicken Vinda–LOOs. Ah, ha, ha, ha.'

I really don't know how we got home. Fortunately he dropped us off and went straight back to London – where he belongs.

Pearl brought down a whole succession of men. None lasted long. She sometimes made it my fault. 'He's not coming down again. You obviously didn't like him.'

I'd never meant to give that impression. If she'd married him I'd've grown to – well, if not like him – tolerate him.

Naturally it was also my fault if I did like one of them. And indeed there was one I found very pleasant. I'd've liked his face and personality reproduced in grandchildren. She never brought him down again.

The very last one – before her workaholic change of heart – and possibly a cause of it – was a drunk. I could see it the moment he walked in, like the mark of Cain. She ignored it. I tried to make light of it. And for a time – before he flaked out – we had a fun meal, one I'd prepared myself and which he really appreciated. It's true that alcohol can bring people together.

I've got into a little routine myself. A glass of wine with dinner. In summer, an aperitif at midday. In winter, a thimbleful of whisky in my early morning coffee. Just civilised living. Nothing more.

After that episode Pearl visited alone. Amber had settled down in University, was doing very well and couldn't spare the time. And Ruby – well, Ruby – she'd nursed a patient back to health, and had fallen for him. The man of her dreams, brought back to life by a good woman's love! She was overjoyed, as if she'd achieved what step-daughterhood might've denied her. She made a very odd request. She wanted the wedding advertised in all the daily papers.

'So Daddy can see I've turned out alright.'

Well, 'Daddy', her father, my husband, had been off the scene for twenty years.

'It ought to go in the local paper,' she assured me, 'in the town he was born. He may have gone back – to spend his later years in familiar territory.'

Huh! Honestly. I ask you. Do people ever go back to – Ipswich? Voluntarily? Almost anywhere else, but surely not Ipswich!

'Do you think he'll come?' she asked. 'In time to give me away?'

Well, darling, I wanted to say, he virtually gave you away – abandoned you – years ago. Along with your two stepsisters. So on balance, without going into all the disputed ins-and-outs, my answer can only be No.

I met him in a pub, must be coming up to twenty-five years ago. He was alone – holding a baby. I wondered how he'd got in that situation. He was young, good-looking. Had he left his wife? Was she dead? In childbirth? Receiving medical care? Something terminal? Or had she given over custody of the child? Been judged, or judged herself, unfit to be a parent? Ended up in prison even?

He must have cottoned on at first glance that I was a soft touch. He said Hello and put the baby in my arms. And then went off to the Gents. Nothing much I could do except hold it. And it was so warm. And fitted so snugly. It looked up to me and smiled. Well, it was probably wind, but I was convinced it had adopted me. I made my mind up to keep it.

He was in that toilet far longer than anyone had a right to be. Then I noticed he was sitting relaxed at the far end of the bar opposite, talking to everyone, and half-way through another pint.

When he re-joined us I didn't ask any searching questions. I flattered him as a father, and showed how knowledgeable and caring I was. Well, with that level of gullibility, anything could happen – and did. And not just then, either. I shouldn't really have been too surprised when two years later – after I'd had two daughters by him in quick succession – that he'd go off, and this time leave me holding all three. It was as if a giant cuckoo, replete with fledgling, had belly-flopped on me, stayed two seasons, laid two eggs and flown the nest. Nice nest – and all that, but …

I got over it. I had no option. But I still tried to conjure up Ruby's mother. Not for her sake, but if her character would come out in the child. Ruby actually looked very like her father, far more so than Pearl or Amber did. So I could only assume the mother was pretty docile and didn't leave much impression behind her. Ruby's placid, too. Takes everything in her stride. When her father left

47

she took it better than the other two. And she's bonded with them very well. I didn't tell them they were half-sisters – not till they'd understand the term and – after fifteen years together – accept it as pretty meaningless. I'd tried to treat them all equally. But for years I actually liked Ruby, the step-child, best. Simply because she was docile and cried less. She became a bit of a goody-two-shoes. Came to want what she'd never experienced – and what I couldn't give her – a quiet marriage, two full-time parents, both biological and no steps. The world desperately needs her type. She performs an extremely important function – sociologically. Bringing up sane, healthy well-balanced children. No chance of a misfit anywhere.

Of course, by the same token, she never had much interest value or story line. So I was quite taken aback when she insisted on contacting her father about the wedding. I hadn't tried to contact him when he walked out on us twenty years ago. So I couldn't see much point her doing so. She was adamant. She drew up the wording of the newspaper advert. It was pretty convoluted, and must have cost a bomb. It boiled down to 'Has anyone seen my father?' No-one had.

The wedding itself went off well. It was just before Christmas and blotted out the need for a seasonal get-together. The four of us had gathered at the church to say goodbye to one of our number.

Of course, we were never all together in one photo. One or other of us had to take it. The happy couple were in every shot. Ruby insisted on sending a photo to the local paper in Ipswich. It was one of the photos I took – and so wasn't in it.

She moved to the other side of town. It could've been the other side of the world the amount I saw her. Amber came down from University even less frequently. Pearl had been very snooty about the wedding 'Puts one off getting married, doesn't it?' She stopped bringing down men. But she still came down regularly.

I'd said to them at the reception, 'I hope to see you all again soon.' They made awkward signs, as if to say, the next get-together will be your funeral. Well, we did all meet together – not at my funeral, though. But at one of theirs.

2

This biography I'm writing of my daughters needed some sort of ending. What I dreaded as a parent proved quite satisfying from a literary angle. It gave the opportunity for a rounded picture of a progeny. I was the first person to see her after her birth. I watched her grow up. I still see the baby in the grown-up, doubt her maturity, even resent the success. True, I wasn't the last person to see her alive. I was given the chance to see her in the coffin. The undertaker wanted me to. 'Our staff have done a wonderful job. She really looks at peace. They're true craftsmen, you know.' Well, perhaps they were. Let them be the last to look on their own handicraft. There are some arts that should be taken on trust, and not have an audience.

As I write the past forms itself into patterns; introduction, themes, counter themes, development, recapitulation, coda – all very musical. And it peaks two-thirds the way along. But the memories don't come back in order. They come unbidden. Difficult to date. They get side-tracked. Ambushed.

How can I make lives for my daughters, and at the same time distance them from my life? And not let that unknown first wife take over and become the main character, the unspoken ideal, who had everything, the whole of received wisdom, good at whatever she tried!

Bringing up three daughters wasn't easy. While they were young how could I have left them at home and gone out to work? I claimed benefits and took a lodger. And when they were at school I retrained so I could work from home. I started as a proof-reader and indexer. I liked that sort of discipline, minute, detailed, precise. I tried to apply it with less success to other routines – tidying, dusting, darning, defrosting. How happily I'd have delegated them to a servant or machine! The indexing was soon overtaken by computers – which actually don't do it so well. But they've opened up other ways of working from home. I learnt new skills. I drew up CVs for the upwardly mobile, trained new businesses to compile reports. I did exam marking, distance learning. I had deadlines, time scales. I tried, as in any other job, to separate 'work time' from 'home time'. But it's not a job in the regular sense. My middle daughter Pearl never considered it work at all. She regarded work as being 'out the house' and with people who spoke the same jargon.

Of course for the purposes of this biography I only use the computer as a high class typewriter. What I now type is more demanding.

Oh, look. There are the squirrels. Two chasing each other. They've stopped to forage. They're fighting over something. Off they go again. I've often seen three together. They're fun to watch, but extremely difficult to tell apart. Other animals have distinctive markings and colours. When they're together, yes, you can compare them by size, dominance, whiteness of the bib, fluffiness of the tail. But singly I can't tell which is which. Or give them pet names.

Fancy that boyfriend of Pearl's saying he'd get a gun to shoot them! Glad she never brought him down again.

In fact, after Ruby's marriage, Pearl's outlook changed. She didn't bring anyone down. She brought down her latest enthusiasms. Which she off-loaded on me. Especially food. She couldn't possibly eat this or that anymore. I wondered if she was ill and had been given a special diet, and was hiding the fact by pretending I was out of date, and always in the wrong. She brought certain items down, claiming they were only available in town. 'Don't mind if I have these, do you? Have one yourself.' Once she brought down a sprig of herbs.

'These will make all the difference.'

'You don't have to tell me. I've got plenty in the garden. Always have had.'

She showed no sign of acknowledging the fact. But she'd registered and, as she always did when contradicted, she later twisted everything to her advantage. She'd never taken any interest in the garden before. As a child she had no inclination towards Nature, except to stamp on dead leaves, and run around in the fresh snow and spoil the picture. But after the herb rebuke she looked out the back window, and let out a long sigh.

'What a mess! That garden's too much for you, isn't it?'

In fact, it was nicely ticking over just the way I wanted. I never made out I was a great gardener. I liked to potter and relax. The plants came up where I put them. No great achievement perhaps, but the preparation and maintenance take up more time than she realised. Pearl couldn't afford a garden in London, not even of those little handkerchiefs you get at the back of terraced houses, still less a patio or roof garden. She began to organise mine.

'You must be careful of your legs, Mother. Varicosity is an omen.'

She treated the established plants as parasites. She was convinced if she pulled them up that everything she planted would automatically spring to life. You should've seen her clearing the undergrowth! Like a thing possessed. Don't ask me to do an imitation of her. You won't catch me grubbing around, stabbing like a wild thing, at every fallen leaf. On manoeuvres she could have been. She kept showing me the scratches on her arm as proof of something or other. Huffing and puffing! What an example she was – better than any man! I wonder sometimes if she felt I'd really wanted a boy.

She tore out the brambles, many of them proper blackberries, which fruited well. She cut down the ivy that was keeping the fence in place. We had a boundary dispute with the neighbour. Legal threats. The fence had to be replaced. I paid, of course.

'Never mind,' Pearl said, 'The neighbours can look over and be jealous.'

'But I don't want Her Next Door looking over.'

'If we have an open plan garden she'll see it at a glance.'

'This isn't an open plan office with glorified houseplants. This is my back garden and I want some privacy.'

'The garden's a mess. It needs to be turned around.'

'What do you mean "turned-around"? A different entrance? A different focal point?'

'Yes,' she mused. 'Possibly that as well.'

And so we had open plan. Out went the little secluded areas, the blind spots that opened out, the corners that smelt of mould and wet leaves. She wouldn't hear of a wild garden or a wilderness.

Just look what she made of it! All at a glance! Twee little compounds, compacted, grave-sized, edged with box boundaries – filled with short stemmed plants packed so tight they stand to attention. Like the grounds of a business college – at conference time. Or a crematorium. All so pat-a-cake. How can you relax? Even the bees have to ask permission to land. And the birds left ages ago. She said I should get the vermin inspector for the squirrels.

And everything had to be accounted for. She kept a pencil behind her ear, like a shop-keeper, and she filled in a note-book as she went along. She often wrote while talking to me, as if she had her mind on other things. She collected the seeds – harvested was the word she used – and put them in marked envelopes. She wanted to sell them, and some of the plants and cuttings.

'This is my back garden,' I protested, 'not a market garden.'

'Money makes the world go round,' she always said.

I always replied, 'And poverty makes it shapeless and flat.' I'm not quite sure what I meant by that, but it always shut her up.

Oh, I grant, it's easier to maintain. A pair of shears and a broom. I prefer a garden that straggles, frayed in cuff and collar, little plants that grow over the path in scallop formations, like edgings of lace, or patternings of lichens. I like a bit of disorder.

And a bit of dirt. Too much cleanliness breaks down your ability to resist disease. Too much order prevents you adapting. She was always too clean for her own good. Dirt pickles you, and builds up your resistance.

It's a way of arranging a garden, I suppose. Not my way. Not the flowers'. But it's a style that comes into fashion every so often. Never lasts long. Burns itself out. Like short hair, you can't do much with it. You have to let it grow to restyle it.

It's not unlike the way she dressed. Immaculate, not a hair out of place. She always chose dresses that were segmented and shaded, sleeves, lapels, bows and pockets. Power dressing. Never stylish, of course, except in an office furniture kind of way. Blue was her favourite colour. Baboon's arse blue.

What could I do? With her? With the garden? She seemed to have a problem leaving the nest. She made the garden her excuse to come down. Every two or three weeks. At first alternating with Amber. I sometimes undid a few of the garden changes and blamed it on Amber.

'What does she know about these things?' queried Pearl. 'Wait till I see her.'

Of course, she never did. Amber's visits tailed off. The first term she'd come home every fortnight, the second every month. I hoped she wasn't falling under any unfortunate influence. Campuses, enclosed communities, estates, always become prey to distasteful things. She changed her course of study, and took up philosophy. Not much practical use. I wondered if she'd ever get a job, or perhaps, as the youngest, stay at home and look after me. Then she said she was going to take a gap year and live, not just travel, abroad.

So, Pearl came down even more. She obviously worked hard in the City and needed to relax, but she disrupted all my routines – or, as she said, lack of routines. The flak I had to put up with. And she expected me to thank her.

'Why don't you …? You could always … Had you ever thought of …? It would pay you if … How would it be if …? You'll never regret it if … If I were you I'd … If you'll be advised by me … Anyone else would have …'

I learned to duck and cringe. I'd been able to take such talk from her – and the other two – when they were girls of thirteen, all bossy and breast-buddy, when they had a new enthusiasm every week and tried to offload it as something original. But for Pearl to go on like this in her twenties! Way beyond the age you should've mellowed and stopped living other people's lives. I never felt scared by her. Just dreaded her coming.

You mustn't think I never answered her back. Or opposed her. I stood up to her. Not as often as I should. She could be very forceful. I once reproved her and said, 'You'll understand when you get to my age.' And added. 'If you ever do.' That shut her up for a time.

'I'm trying to help you,' she continued later. 'The garden is physical work. I know how you must feel at your time of life.'

I knew what she was getting at. Or I thought I did. I didn't take it seriously. I had no reason to. She never talked about personal things. She'd become quite proper. She had only once stayed here overnight with one of her men friends. That was the only time I ever heard her swear – and it wasn't totally inappropriate to the situation.

I'd been polite and understanding and shown no surprise when the two of them were still around at bed-time. I went to bed early and let them get on with it. I got up early to show willing and prepare breakfast for them both. Pearl came down far earlier than I anticipated.

'Where's your friend?' I asked.

'He went.'

'He must have gone off very early.'

'Yes, I sent him away at daybreak. There was no way that cock was going to crow a second time.'

I remember dropping something. It must've been onto the carpet. It made no noise. She didn't seem to hear. We went on talking as if nothing had happened.

Later that day – and she didn't leave as early as she usually did – she yawned and said, 'It's vastly over-estimated, isn't it? I can quite see why you get on so happily without it.'

That was when I began to wonder about her. All those men

54

she'd brought down. She paraded them as if trying to establish something. Not just proving she could get as many as she liked. Not just for me to approve her choice. It was beyond that. They were all her age – the age when I married – and they all resembled, one way or another, my husband, her father. As if she was touting for me! Tempting me to make a fool of myself. How she'd have loved it if I had.

'Mother. Really! At your age! You should know better.'

Had I really been under scrutiny? Did she come down simply to help in the garden? And the real reason she went round the garden with a pencil and notebook? It wasn't to jot things down about the plants, was it? No. For all her pretence that she was paying me only half attention she was in fact studying me intently and taking notes. Adding them to the file she'd compiled on my reactions to her men 'friends'. Charting the development of what she saw fit to call my 'illness'?

Farcical, but it fitted in. And then, all-unbidden, I had this appalling dream. I'd never had one for years. Which I suppose made it even more distasteful. It was my birthday. She came down with a present, and gave it to me with that same smug look she had when introducing her friends.

'I've written a book about you, Mother.'

'You've written a book … about … me?'

'Yes. Why not?'

'And you've had it published?'

'Yes. That's what's in the parcel. Open it.'

I can remember a rustling noise. It started with the blood pumping behind my ears. It grew louder and louder as if a herd of cows was charging through the undergrowth. I took off the last sheet of wrapping paper. The book was called "Mummy's Menopause."

I could hardly draw breath, let alone speak.

'I hope you're not offended,' she said. 'I had to use the word Mummy. Mother wouldn't have sounded quite so good. I do hope you don't think I'm being familiar in any way, Mother.'

Familiar? Familiar? Your own Mother's Menopause – under her own Daughter's Microscope. Blow by blow. Drip by drip. Familiar? Oh, no. No. Think nothing of it.

She'd been dwelling on my private life – and the private life of parents is as near I get to admitting the existence of a taboo.

'I wrote it to help my generation know what to avoid.'

'What to …?'

'In particular your performance – and your moods.'

'I don't work – and I don't have moods.'

'You're not the easiest person to get on with, are you? My generation will nevertheless thank you for showing them …'

'… what to avoid! So they don't turn out like me.' Very calmly I added, 'And would never be capable of doing what I am about to do.'

And with that I returned the compliment and tried to push the book up where it belonged. Yes, I attempted to rape my own daughter with the book she'd written about my menopause. The hardback edition, too.

When I woke to my own screams I knew in the back of my mind that something awful – in real life – was going to happen. I couldn't get the dream – and her motivation – out of my mind. I wanted to rid myself of it. Of her, too. I wanted her out of my life. Right out.

Then I got the message from her workplace. My first reaction was guilt. Had I got special powers? To commit infanticide from a distance? And be undetected?

What a gift! Too often it's the children who write biographies of their dead parents – without having shared the subject's early life. It's a marvellous situation – from a literary point of view – to be able to chart a life all the way through. Perhaps not one hundred percent objective, of course. But let's face it, who else would want to write about her? Relatives have some uses. What should I call my book? How about? "My Daughter – Start to Finish."

Yes, if you've got any nagging resentments about your children – if they're successful and rich – do encourage them to predecease you. It's the best way for them to provide for your old age. If they live, they'll only put you in a home. Murder stories used to be about children trying to bump off their rich parents. Why not about poor parents doing in their rich children? Would make such a change from the usual victims – parents, old ladies, maiden aunts. I'll have to copyright that. Write one myself. Might sell better than the biography I'm writing.

That said, I don't think children's rights should be extended to the freedom to predecease parents. It makes the parents feel guilty. As if it really should have been them. It puts pressure on them to follow suit quickly. Well, I'm sorry … in my case … can't speak for yours … I don't feel obliged to …

She'd phoned the previous weekend to say she mightn't be coming down. Then she phoned again to say she would, but had a cold and didn't want me to catch the germs. Usually it was a case of her not wanting to be contaminated by me. Indeed the only way I could ever stop her coming down was by saying, 'I've got flu.'

It was more than a cold she had. When she arrived she was exhausted. She said she'd keep out of my way. She insisted on gardening, despite the weather. I made myself scarce indoors, in the warm. She did whatever, and on Sunday morning she went back. On Thursday I had the news.

At some meeting apparently. Very public. She got all worked up over a minor point of order, and in a kind of spontaneous combustion – self-destructed. They gave her artificial respiration, banged her chest, called an ambulance, but she was Dead on Arrival.

There was an autopsy. And for a time they said the cause of death was an affection of the heart. Affection! What a word – for a disease. Affection.

> 'Doctor, doctor, tell me please
> Is it love or heart disease?'

The word they finally came up with was Syncope. Fainting really – but you can die from it. A temporary loss of blood supply to the brain, especially when you stand up quickly or for too long. It can be brought on by stress. Seemingly, it's often hereditary and can bypass – miss a beat between – generations. She had it. Presumably I – and her father – do not.

When I heard the news I couldn't absorb it. I just wanted to pass it on like salacious gossip. 'Who else can I tell?' Well, Amber was abroad on her gap year and difficult to contact. Ruby's phone was out of order. I couldn't bring myself to cross town, and so wrote a letter.

I could have done with a bit of support. I panicked. Who else was there to tell? Well, there was her father. True he hadn't been heard of over twenty years but even so … We might be required to trace him if he were mentioned in the will. There's no reason he should be. There might be no will. Still, we couldn't just tell him about the money, and not about her death.

I did what I should have done twenty odd years before. I surprised myself in doing so. I went to a private detective and explained the circumstances. He was not very sympathetic.

'A bit late, isn't it? Funny thing to do – trace your husband when your daughter dies. You're not in some way trying to call her back, through him?'

'No.'

'Or him through … ?'

'Just do what I ask.'

'Are you sure you need a private investigator? And not a counsellor?'

'You will be paid.'

Looking back, well … I don't know what I was thinking. I lost my head. I should've been lamenting my daughter. Could his departure after all this time rankle more? Does humiliation cut deeper than bereavement? It revived all the speculation. Had he gone back to his first wife? Married again? Started a new family?

I didn't hear from him when he left me thirty years ago, nor twenty-five years later when Ruby got married. It was ridiculous to suppose … a bizarre thing to expect. It showed the state of my mind.

But, as luck would have it, on this occasion, there was a result. I received a letter from someone who claimed to be − God, not another one! − his daughter! He'd died only a few weeks earlier. She apologised for not having made contact. The signature was illegible. I couldn't tell if he'd named her after a gemstone as well. There was no address, and I couldn't read the postmark. I'm pretty sure it wasn't Ipswich.

The problem should at long last have been put to rest. But now we had two deaths. Ruby received my letter and made a dramatic appearance.

'Oh God. She was younger than me.'

'Yes, and I've got some more news for you. Your father …'

I showed her the letter. She asked to keep it.

'He was my only biological relative. That means something, doesn't it? I know you can't fully understand, of course.'

'I was only his wife,' I said.

'I'll get over it,' she said.

'I have.'

And so did Amber when she finally got back from abroad. She rounded on Ruby.

'Fancy worrying about him! Honestly. So many years on. Talk about living in the past. What about poor Pearl?'

And yet Amber, too, was strangely unmoved. 'I hated her opinions,' she said. 'She was just a money-maker. I know she was my sister. Not that that's everything. Ruby is my half-sister. I love her as much. Blood isn't everything. She wasn't my sister-in-arms.'

'No, dear,' I said, 'I don't suppose she was.' I assumed this was her way of diminishing the grief.

She began to call me by my first name. I didn't object. It made us feel equal and closer. It was typical of her. Pearl would never have countenanced such a thing. It would never have occurred to Ruby.

Pearl's boss phoned. He sounded very sympathetic. He wanted to sort out some personal effects she'd left in her office desk.

'I understand,' I said. 'I expect you need the space for her replacement to move in?'

'Actually, when she died we took the opportunity of abolishing the post.'

I never knew much about her job. I heard about the workload, meetings, travel, stress, promotion prospects – but not what she actually did. Apparently her firm had a finger in almost every type of business, in every part of the world. It had hit the headlines for a different reason. It planned to extend its London premises onto an adjacent site. A record sum was paid to outbid rivals. When the old building was knocked down the foundations of an even older one were discovered, a medieval market, a storehouse and market cross. Building work was delayed a week for an archaeological survey. There was a public outcry, with demonstrations led by celebrity this, celebrity that. Under pressure the firm agreed to relocate the old market – every beam, brick and stone – and reconstruct it within the main foyer of the new building. In one of those enormous vaults, several stories high, all glass – what do you call them? – narthex, atrium.

At the grand opening there was a small exhibition. How was it billed? "Respecting the Past. From street market to international free-flow of capital. A continuum." All the celebrities who'd previously demonstrated turned up for the plonk and mousetrap. The following weekend Pearl came down – full of it.

'You like the past, Mother. You should see what the firm's done to make it relevant.'

'I saw it on TV.'

'No, you need to see it in the flesh.'

I was invited to view the exhibition. I arrived early morning. Only limited openings to the public now. The spotlights had gone and the old building looked gloomy.

 Pearl pulled me to the reconstructed market cross and pointed to the underside of the roof.

'Look. There they are. Can you see mine? There.' She was dancing around like a little girl.

I could barely see anything. I wasn't sure what I was looking for. Then I realised that every stone and brick and beam had names carved on them.

'See mine. Up there. Can you see it?

Frankly all the plaques – they were tiles really, arranged herringbone fashion, so you had to twist your neck to align with the writing – were indistinguishable. It was like finding your fledgling in a gannet colony.

'Oh, yes,' I lied.

'We had to pay a fortune for these. But worth it, don't you think?'

'You mean you paid to have your name inscribed on a …?'

'Yes. We had the choice of beam, brick or stone? And in three different type-faces. The staff had priority.'

'So your firm didn't actually pay for the reconstruction?'

'They planned it all and advertised it – but it had to be financed.'

I didn't like to ask if the position of the plaque corresponded to the amount donated.

'Mine looks better in the midday sun. Let's look at the rest then you can take a photo.'

She dragged me round the reconstructed market, forever stressing the continuity of trade and commerce. I suppose she had a point – an old market pushing its wares with street cries isn't dissimilar to advertising and jingles. And she herself, as she made point after point, stood defiantly, with her hands on her hips, like a Hamburg fish-wife.

'Come, the sun's moved over. Time for the photo. Take me. Take me.'

I couldn't possibly fit her and the plaque into one shot. It would've been difficult enough to take the plaque by itself without a flash and zoom. All we managed was her pointing upwards. She was delighted with the result.

That was the only contact I had with her work. As far as I'm concerned that plaque's her memorial One brick out of thousands – just a name, no dates – and in a building of conjectural, indeed, dubious accuracy.

I'm happy to leave the memorial there – and keep the photograph here. In a prominent place. On my writing desk. Not a bad photo, I suppose. It's almost more inspirational not to know what she's pointing at!

Amber asked me about it. I never told her about the plaque. She would have gone off alarming.

'What's she pointing at?'

'Some rare, migratory bird – or other. Landed on some old building. Or other.'

Flew into my life. Then left it for good.

3

How could I have known whether Pearl wanted to be buried or cremated? Scattered in the garden or interred in one of those little six-by-two flower beds, edged with box? A decision had to be made. I went by her own rule of life – I shopped around and opted for the cheapest.

Yet at the same time I wanted everything to pass off smoothly. I couldn't bear the thought of a hitch or mishap. I had to live up to her own presumed efficiency. I felt obliged to tell Ruby that I'd really prefer she didn't bring her children to the funeral. They might disturb the proceedings. They were far too young anyway. I wasn't sure how she'd react. If she contested the point I'd snap down a clincher – to the effect that 'Pearl hated children.' And if this didn't work I'd have added, 'And yours, most of all.' As it happened Ruby didn't respond. She said nothing, just smiled. Almost as if she didn't feel the need to reply. Or had some trump of her own up her sleeve.

I had the feeling she was determined to prove a point. At my expense. It took me some time to figure out what it might be. Was it that letter? The one that confirmed my husband's death, the one from his alleged other daughter? That letter had more effect on Ruby than Pearl's death. Did the prospect of a replacement step-sister cushion the gap? So, tell me, did she employ a detective agency to trace this other daughter? Like I'd done to trace the father? Understandably in my case. Pointlessly in hers. This 'new' daughter wasn't a missing person. No one knew of her existence. And she obviously didn't want to make contact or leave details. So why should Ruby take it upon herself to …? OK, she's every right if she chooses – and pays. But really! Does she have to seek a substitute? So soon? So distant? Oh, God, she's not going to invite her to the funeral, is she? And justify it on the basis that they all had the same father? And that they were named after gem stones. Well, they didn't all have the same mother. Pearl and Amber did. One's dead, and you can leave the other one out the reckoning. That leaves two to compare notes. What was your mother like, eh? No, don't tell me. I don't want to know. Do I? Might I? If Ruby can set about tracing her erstwhile sister, then like as not she's already traced her real mother! My husband's first wife. So, can I expect to see her at funeral as well? Arriving late. Skulking at the back. In the half light. Behind the pillars.

The funeral went off without incident. There were several people from Pearl's office, and two of the men she'd brought down. I invited them back to the house but neither came. Ruby who had been separated from her children for all of three hours rushed off, with two slices of cake wrapped in doilies.

Amber helped me clear up. She was a great comfort to me. We sorted through some of Pearl's belongings. She selected a couple of small mementoes to take back.

'Aren't you going to wait for the will?' I said.

'I can't imagine her leaving me anything. No reason why she should. I'm not interested.'

4

I didn't expect to hear from Ruby for some time. I'd obviously offended her. Poor woman! She couldn't conceive of anyone not wanting to be surrounded by her children. However, a few days after the funeral she phoned as if nothing had happened, pleasant as pie, suspiciously so. That's right, dear. Polish that halo. You've forgiven me for not allowing them to the funeral. So what am I supposed to say? They're welcome to come to mine?

'Do pop over,' she said. 'The children'd love to see you. They'll cheer you up.'

I had other ways of cheering myself.

A week later her husband phoned and tried to jolly me along, like some cheerleader from a holiday camp.

'Do come over. They'll be a tonic.'

Not my kind of tonic. I don't like too much tonic. Drowns the real pleasure.

I liked the grandchildren well enough – as a conversational ploy when all else failed. But not the other rôles they're supposed to fulfil. Occasional company, no real responsibility. I wasn't into buying them off, giving them treats and presents their parents would've frowned on. And as for the rejuvenation factor! I've never wanted to relive my childhood through grandchildren. Small they may be, but they cover a lot of ground, get everywhere and make far too much noise. Not my idea of rejuvenation at all. In fact, they remind me of elephants, yes, elephants. The male elephant tries to bring dying female back to life by mounting her. Last thing you bloody want!

'Katie kicked her first football last week.'

64

'And Holly's just got her first tooth. She's been so brave. I didn't really need to stay up with her every night this week. But I'm glad I did.'

I didn't need cheering up. I didn't want to be seen as the mother in excelsis, suffering beyond the call of duty, beyond the natural span of human affection, ennobled by a pre-decease. I wanted to get away from being a Mother. I'd always sworn that when my daughters left home I'd look up all the friends I had before marriage. That was a long time ago. I've lost contact. And I'm not going to get a detective to trace them!

I did nose a bit over the fence to see what the neighbours were up to. The one on the left – she's been widowed for years – has a vast network of friends. They're always having parties, smelly barbecues, wine tasting evenings, going off to the theatre. It gets her out of the house. She never had children herself. I think most of her friends are single, or only children.

And the one on the right, well, we met by chance in the High Street. She put her arm round me and gushed.

'I don't see you so much in the garden now. She made it so perfect, didn't she? If ever I have a bad day I look out my back window and think wouldn't it be lovely if the whole world was like that – ordered, patterned, nothing out of place, worthy to contemplate! You must maintain it. Don't let it go to seed.'

What she really meant was don't let yourself go to seed. I'm made of sterner stuff than that. But the garden's welcome to revert. Soon as it likes. Let the edges mellow. Let the plants self-seed. A bit of weeding here, planting bulbs there. It'll revert by itself. Won't need tending.

Which wasn't the case with the house. I toyed with moving somewhere smaller. I didn't need the spare bedrooms. Pearl was gone, and Amber's room was rarely used. What was the point?

And then the probate came through. Pearl never made a proper will, but indicated everything should come to me. She'd put most of her money in shares, dozens of different companies, relatively small amounts, tied up for years to come. That still left a tidy sum in ready cash. I saw no reason to give any to Amber. She'd said she didn't want any. She wasn't that sort of person. Ruby was. But she had her husband to look after her. They'd get whatever in due course.

I decided to stay. And redecorate and renovate. Not a makeover, just enough to see me out. The man who surveyed the house and drew up the estimates said I was sitting on a goldmine. There was nothing wrong with the wiring, waterworks or woodwork. No damp, no beetles. He suggested a bit of fine tuning here and there, a lick of paint throughout, and an upgrade in the kitchen and bathroom.

'No,' I thought, 'I want something more than that.'

It began with extra wiring for wall lamps. Then a partition wall removed. Then a picture window in the wall that overlooked the back garden. Then no wall at all but a conservatory, a proper one, not a lean-to. The size of a lounge, with power points and plumbing.

The time it seemed to take! The noise, the dirt, the disruption! I draped the furniture with sheets, packed away the china, and decamped to one of the spare bedrooms, took all I needed and virtually lived in a bed-sit in my own home.

Five times a day I came down. To let the workmen in, to make morning coffee, coffee at lunchtime, afternoon tea, and at the end of their day for a progress report. I could put up with the sounds of banging and drilling as I knew exactly what was happening. The workmen always tidied up afterwards. They were always appreciative of their mugs of tea and coffee. Cheery, reliable, uncomplicated men, they were. I missed them when they finished. It took them far less time than I expected, almost a wand-wave transformation in a matter of weeks.

When they'd gone I'd come downstairs in the morning and think, 'What do I need all this space for?' Bit by bit I grew into it. I think it's quite important to have a separate dining room from the lounge – though in good weather the conservatory serves as both.

News got around that I'd inherited and redecorated. The neighbour on the right developed a neck like a giraffe and a nose like a tapir. Then Ruby made an appearance.

'Oh, Mother, I'm so sorry that we haven't been able to see you for so long – but you know how it is – with children.'

'I think you might have called. You are on the phone.'

'Not any more. We had to get rid of the landline. And I know you don't like mobiles. Of course, we've been anxious about you. All alone in this big house. We've been so pre-occupied. I'm doing extra hours at work now. The money doesn't go as far as it did.'

'I know that as well as anyone, dear.'

'Yes, but you don't have a young family.'

'Not any more, no. But you've always managed before.'

'Yes, but you see. There's another one on the way.'

I was surprised. She'd always sworn she wasn't going to have any more. Yet it explained a lot of things. Had she known she was pregnant when Pearl died? And not liked to tell me? And when I said I didn't want her children at the funeral, and she gave me that odd look, had she known what an impossible request I was making? No way could she not take her unborn child along with her to the funeral. Strange outcome that. Bad omen.

'I'm pleased for you. There'll be quite a gap between them, won't there? Did you keep the prams and cots? They'll come in useful, won't they?'

'Well, actually, we didn't. It was a surprise to us, as you can imagine.'

'I can, yes.'

'And the expense is going to be enormous. Of course, if it's a girl she can share the girls' bedroom, but if it's a boy – and we do so much want a boy …'

'Yes, I can understand that.'

'… then we'll need an extra room.'

I paused, sensed something in the air and said, 'There are some lovely houses going up on that new development the other end of town. The advertisement says they're architect designed.'

'Yes, but they're lovely prices as well. We've hunted everywhere. We're quite exhausted.'

I said nothing but anticipated.

'Mummy. I'm so glad you've had the house redecorated. We thought perhaps you wanted to keep it exactly as it was ... when ... to remind yourself ... of ... But obviously you've adapted. Would you ... ?'

'Yes?'

'Would you be prepared ... ?'

'Go on.'

'To have the upstairs altered – made into a flat? It would be just the right size for us. We'd keep ourselves to ourselves. Have it self-contained. It's such a big house. Just for one. We'd pay you well. Wouldn't interfere. Honestly, Mum.'

I noted the conjugation Mother, Mummy, Mum. I smiled at her.

'What about Amber? She'll be back after her gap year.'

'Will she? Surely she could stay on the settee. She's probably got used to sleeping rough where she is anyway. She'll understand. She's single.'

'I'm single, too, dear. I'm not sure I do understand.' I brought myself to say what I'd never said before. 'What if I met someone I wanted to live with? It's not impossible. Is it allowable? Even the thought of it?'

Ruby gave me a funny look. You know how people can give a funny look even with their eyes lowered.

'When's the baby due?' I asked.

'In about five months.'

'I'd love to see it, especially if it's a boy.'

Ruby got up to go.

'You'll be coming around again soon, won't you, dear?'

'I shall be very busy as you'll appreciate.'

'You won't stay for tea? You're very welcome. I always take some at this time. It's a habit I got into when the decorators were here.'

'No, I must go. Goodbye, Mother.'

The tea was delicious. I drank it out the best set, cup after cup.

Of course, she thought I refused her because she was the step-daughter. She'd have been wrong – I didn't want any of them here – singly, with family or liaisons. Though, I might have got on with Amber. She could have read her philosophy books and looked after me.

The next I heard from Ruby was by letter. "We've decided to emigrate. It's best for us. I hope you won't try to dissuade us. We've chosen to go to New Zealand. People say it's like this country was thirty years ago."

I was surprised. I didn't think she had it in her. Apparently her husband's father had spent time there when a young man. I assumed she'd contact me before she left. Then I got a postcard. They were already there. Living in a bungalow on the slopes of an extinct volcano.

"The lava flow of thousands of years ago has made the soil very fertile. We've got two sheep and we're growing all our own food."

Big deal!

"And it really is just like it used to be back there thirty years ago!"

How could she know? She wasn't born thirty years ago. What a stupid remark! What was I doing thirty years ago? What could I – what should I have been doing? A good age to be, but not if the clock has to go back as well. Who was in power then?

I assumed she'd tell me when the baby was born. A couple of months later I had a phone call. A woman's voice said –

'I've a message from your daughter.'

That's it. I thought. She's 'ad it. Bit premature, but … at least she's thought to tell me.

It wasn't about Ruby. It concerned Amber.

'Is there any problem?'

'She's fine,' said the voice. 'She has a message for you. I'd like to deliver it personally.'

It was Amber's former flat mate from University. We arranged a visit. I assumed it was to deliver a present that would have been too heavy, costly or fragile to send from abroad.

The girl looked just like she did in the photo.

'Amber's decided she isn't going back to University.'

'Oh. Did she tell you why?'

'She's come across things in her gap year which have made University seem inappropriate.'

'Things! Oh, dear. I never really believed in gap years. You lose continuity. What's she going to do when she gets back?'

'She isn't coming back. She says she sees the world from a different angle now. Family doesn't mean so much these days. Nothing personal. She thinks of you as a friend and supporter in her formative years. She thinks of everyone as a brother and sister – in the fight for justice. In the world situation today, she says, there can be no figures of authority, and no conflict between the generations. Her work keeps her out there – and the people around her are her new family.'

'I suppose I can see that. I think. Coming from her.'

'She says she knows you'll understand. She says she's sorry it's through me. Second hand.'

'Oh, no. It's good of you. Very noble of her.'

'It's word for word, I assure you.'

'I don't doubt that.'

No, I didn't doubt the message had been correctly relayed. I could almost hear Amber saying it. In retrospect it fitted in, though not to the extent of being predictable. I went over the words. I couldn't forget them. I could hear her saying them.

"Family doesn't mean so much these days. Nothing personal. I think of you as a friend and supporter in my formative years. Now I think of everyone as a brother and sister – in the fight for justice. In the world situation today there can be no figures of authority, and no conflict between the generations."

'It's a blow to me, as well,' said her friend. 'I really admire what she's doing. She's more courageous than me. I'm not the person for it. We were like twins at College. It's the parting of the ways for us. They used to call us Amber and Esme, the gem twins. Not the Gemini twins, the gem twins.'

'Why?' I forced myself to ask.

'We were both named after gemstones. Esme is short for Esmeralda – Spanish for emerald.'

'I see. I think. Perhaps I don't. And Esme, tell me – are you going back?'

'No, I'm here for good. Amber asked me to keep in touch with you. I'm not going to write to her – there's no proper communication, anyway. But she wants me to keep an eye on you. She asked me always to come in person.'

'That's very nice of her, I suppose. And, of you.'

'When can I come round next?'

'Shall I contact you?'

'You won't forget, will you? Here's my number. I did promise her. I won't always talk about her. Promise.'

She looked at me. Like a surrogate daughter. I really don't want any more. Three was quite enough.

I've only got the past to go on now. Which means there can be some sort of ending.

I'm under no pressure to move house, but I'm considering going. I don't suppose I will. I have their joint biography to finish. I've got all the material I'm ever going to get. There won't need to be a revised edition.

The Untoward Invention

The Untoward Invention

Hoddinott had been a dustman originally. He'd taken the job knowing full well it was below his capabilities. He hoped some more congenial work might come his way. He'd pursued it often enough without success. He wasn't called up during the War owing to an injured knee. In his part of London bombs destroyed most of the garbage as well as many of the houses. What was left of either was cleared by bulldozers. The Labour Exchange advised there were vacancies in sewage. If he didn't mind the hazards – the filth and the risk of infection – he could start as soon as he liked.

'No,' thought Hoddinott. 'I'm used to filth and infection, and prefer rats to blue-bottles.'

He spent twenty years in sewage, first down the sewers, next on a plant as labourer, foreman, and then as public relations manager. He took parties of visitors round the plant, showing them how the sewage was processed and the water purified. At the end of each tour he gave them a glass of the water to drink. He laughed to himself as he watched them gingerly sip the water. How many lungfuls of putrid stench had he inhaled? How many inadvertent mouthfuls of sludge? Finally – when his knee began to play up so much that the tours became impossible – he was transferred to a sedentary job in the Scientific Branch. And there, at last, he found the work more in line with his capabilities.

However, he was forced by ill-health to retire early. He retained full pension rights and was able to purchase the small home that had been provided by the works, number 21 Outfall Alley. It was a pleasant enough house and satisfied his needs. Nothing grew in the garden – twenty years earlier he'd hoped to grow outsize vegetables, but humans aren't even good at producing effective manure. The only thing to do with human waste is to dispose of it. Hoddinott used his garden shed for experiments to do just that. Nothing so elaborate as the Scientific Branch, of course, but in its way ingenious.

The aim of his experiments was to filter and purify. Then a jet of flame would burn as much as possible, and then draw in the rest, without any dust escaping, to a cavity surrounding the original source of flame. Finally this residue would be emptied and disposed of appropriately. Hoddinott considered that such a plan would be feasible on a large scale. It would prove cheap, efficient, labour-saving and beneficial to all mankind. His enthusiasm was such that he allowed his house to go to ruin, and impaired his own precarious health by rising early and working into the small hours. The garden shed was the centre of operations. And it was there, one night, in the most inauspicious of circumstances, that he brought to birth the fruit of his labours.

It was past Friday midnight, first thing Saturday morning, and three youths, back from a stag party, were struggling along the maze-like streets of the estate. Two of them were mouthing obscenities at the third, Jed, who was to be married that morning. All three were drunk, lost, and in need of somewhere to relieve themselves. The houses had no front gardens; the front doors opened onto the pavements. The suggestion that the letter-boxes were the right height was discountenanced by the intermittent barking of dogs.

'There's a dark place here,' one said, pointing to Hoddinott's house.

'Yeah, round the back.'

The three trooped into the back garden. There were no trees.

'Up the wall.'

'Up the overflow.'

Hoddinott was deeply engrossed in the finishing touches of a pocket-sized version of the invention that he hoped might one day materialise into a full-scale industrial complex. The noises outside disturbed him. He turned off the lamp, picked up his disposal gun, as a mother picks up a new-born baby in danger, opened the door and called out –

'Who's there?'

His voice startled the three youths. Jed, who was at the garden wall, finished first and all too hastily pulled up his zip. The blood-curdling yelp he let out convinced Hoddinott that the intruder was not human. He instinctively pulled the trigger. Five seconds elapsed. A human silhouette hoisted itself over the wall, then – in a blinding flash of white light – disappeared.

'Good God,' Hoddinott thought. 'I've killed someone.'

The sound of running footsteps reassured him. He looked over the fence. He could see nothing. The footsteps, now two distinct pairs, were retreating fast. Further investigation with a torch revealed no sign of a body, but a gap in the wall.

'My God! I have killed somebody. The gun works. It works.'

Torn between horror and delight Hoddinott retreated to the shed. His intention had been to test his disposal gun on some inanimate object, and then, if the invention worked, take it to the Patents Office. His only course of action now was to take himself to the nearest police station.

'So what happened to Jed?' said one of the youths as they turned the far corner of Outfall Alley.

'Got away over the garden wall, didn't he?'

'But what was that flash?'

'Dunno. Let's get home.'

In their sobered state they found their way back to the flat they shared. Jed's clothes for the morning were hanging on the picture rail.

'He won't be long.'

'Unless he's been caught.'

'They'll soon release him.'

77

They lay on their beds exhausted and fell asleep.

Hoddinott went into the Police Station and rang at the reception desk.

'Sit down a minute, please,' said the Desk Sergeant, a telephone at one ear, a pencil stuck over the other.

'But it's very urgent.'

'So's this. I've got an emergency here. Someone's just been run over by an ambulance.'

'Oh,' said Hoddinott. It seemed an eternity before the Sergeant was free.

'Nasty business that,' the policeman said, dusting his hands together. 'Someone's for the high jump. Only last week two of our police cars collided. You should have heard the language. Couldn't do anything, though. The drivers were the same rank. They still are,' he added reflectively, 'only lower.'

'What I've got to say is very important,' interrupted Hoddinott.

'Of course. Now, sir, your name, please, your abode, if fixed, and your occupation, if any, on this form.'

'Is that necessary at the moment?'

'It's the first thing we want to know, sir. Write it legibly, please. We spend half the day trying to decipher handwriting. It might be good training for an MI5 detective trying to break codes, but for a Station Sergeant it's less than useless. Yes, that's legible enough. Thank you, Mr Hardinut.'

'Hoddinott.'

'Oh, I beg your pardon. Now what's your problem?'

'I've just killed someone.'

The Sergeant, who was about to correct the name on the form, put down the pen.

'And how did you come to do that, sir?'

'With my ray gun.'

'With your ray gun? Oh, I see.' The Sergeant paused and picked up his pen. 'Before we go any further, sir, would you like to add the name and address of your doctor? Just a formality, you understand. That's right. Legibly as before. Now, sir, who was it you killed?'

'I don't know.'

'Well, give a brief description.'

'I can't.'

'Didn't the person in question have any peculiarities? Most people have. They don't think they have … but they do.' He gave a significant look at Hoddinott, who shook his head. 'No peculiarities. That's a peculiarity in itself. We'll have to identify the body ourselves. Where is it?'

'There isn't one.'

'There's always a body, sir. In a case like this. I've dealt with so many. If you've killed someone there's always – unless, of course. How long ago was this?'

'Tonight.'

'Then there must be a body.'

'No, because I used my ray gun.'

'So you said.'

'You see my ray gun kills and disposes at the same time.'

'Does it now? That's very interesting?'

'So there's no evidence of a crime at all. That's what I'm worried about.'

'It's worrying me a bit, too. Are you sure there was a crime? Because I've better things to do …'

'Yes, officer. There was a crime.'

'Any witnesses?'

'There were two others.'

'Description,' the Sergeant asked, raising his pen hopefully.

'I only heard the footsteps.'

'Did they commit a crime?'

'I don't know. They ran off. They were trespassing, you see.'

The Sergeant leaned over the desk, hoping to catch a whiff of alcohol. He smiled at Hoddinott. 'Say something, sir.'

'I'm sorry. What did you say?'

'Forget it.' The Sergeant drummed his fingers on the counter top and summoned a thought.

'Do you regard yourself as a criminal, sir?'

'Alas, yes.'

'Would you mind spending the rest of the night in a cell? And we can check the details in the morning.'

'Certainly, Officer. Which way is it?'

Hoddinott was locked in. He lay down, relieved he'd admitted his crime. The Sergeant phoned through to the Superintendent and explained the situation. The reply came –

'Keep him there as long as you can. Phone his doctor. Check the Missing Persons Files. If nothing new comes up in the next few days, drop it. Hang on, though. Better ask to see the ray gun. And if there is one, confiscate it. In fact to be on the safe side I'll give you a Search Warrant for his house. You never know with these nut cases. Hardinut seems an appropriate name.'

Jed's wedding was timed for 11 o'clock Saturday morning. He'd planned down to the last detail, despite misgivings about the whole concept of marriage, and an intense dislike of his fiancée's mother. He'd even set the alarm clock for 8.30am, enough time to get ready, not enough time to start worrying. It woke his flat mates.

'Here, look. His bed hasn't been slept in.'

'Maybe he's a light sleeper,' yawned the other.

'Serious. Look. It's not even creased.'

'Perhaps he went over to her place.'

'They wouldn't have that. He's been caught, that's what. We'll have to bail him out.'

'No, better phone the police station first.'

They phoned and were told that no-one had been imprisoned overnight except an elderly man. They looked at one another, realising they had the sorry duty of telling Jed's fiancée of his disappearance.

'I never thought he'd go through with it anyway.'

'She wasn't worth it. Still she didn't deserve this. He might have warned us.'

'Can't help admiring him.'

Hoddinott's house was searched, and nothing was found. A keen, young detective insisted on searching the garden shed and there he found the strange object Hoddinott called his 'ray gun'.

'My God, is that it?'

The Station Sergeant stooped down and picked it up – an act which shocked the Detective for there would be 'a superimposition of fingerprints'.

'You shouldn't have picked that up without gloves,' he censured. 'And it might be dangerous.'

'Wonder how it works?' the Sergeant said, ignoring him. 'Something obviously comes out of this end and you pull this thing, I suppose.' He aimed the gun at a potted geranium and pulled the trigger.

Both Sergeant and Detective were silenced by a twanging noise, a flash of light and the sudden and complete disappearance of the geranium.

Dazed and cowed the Detective muttered, 'Refer to Higher Authority.'

Higher Authority in the form of the Station Superintendent referred the matter to the Ministry of Defence where it eventually found its way to the appropriate section.

'It's of no great use militarily – as yet,' said the Brigadier, Chief of Army Secret Scientific Research. 'Because, you see, like a gun it's discriminating. Can only be used against individuals. Could be used against the civilian population – getting rid of potential enemies, for instance. No chance of that in this country, of course. Thank God.'

The Minister of Defence changed the line of discussion and turned to the Brigadier's Top Scientific Adviser. 'How does it work?'

'Pressurised heat basically,' the Scientist said. 'It operates on three levels at once – that's the beauty of it, even if, as the Brigadier says, it's of no great use. First, it sucks in all the air from the body, and uses it again. This means there's no scream from the victim because the lungs are emptied. Second, intense heat enters the vacuum so that the body, which is ninety percent water anyway, is cremated there and then. Finally the sheer force of the jet disperses the dust, so that there is little trace at all. There is a modification in the inventor's plan for sucking back the minute residue – quite how this would've worked I'm not sure. As it now stands little trace is left. There is a white flash. And then nothing.'

'You see,' said the Brigadier, rubbing his hands, 'There is no burial, no drama, no anguished faces, no gestures, no blood, no pity of it all.'

The Minister felt a lump in his throat. 'Even the most squeamish person can use it without feeling bad?'

'Not entirely, no,' said the Brigadier sadly. 'There is one drawback. A fault in the design. When the trigger's pulled it makes a noise, like a mournful chord on a cello. It could sap confidence. Might make the man with the gun feel a bit – off.'

'Can it be eradicated?'

'Would have thought so,' said the Scientist. 'One would hardly call it sophisticated yet.'

'You say just a slight noise and a flash?'

'The flash is fairly bright. It's advisable to turn your eyes away.'

'But there's no means of detection? Or finding out if – er – anything's happened?'

'No. We tested it on a police dog. Even the studs on its collar disappeared.'

'Then gentlemen,' the Minister said, 'this invention could have profound consequences on any number of issues.'

'Very true, Minister. We thought you should see it as soon as we realised its full potential.'

'Full potential? Quite right, Brigadier. You did quite right there. I'll have to tell the Prime Minister. Make a full report. Top secret, of course.'

He walked out feeling slightly ill, but clear of his duty in the matter.

'I say,' the Brigadier said to his Scientific Adviser, 'this weapon destroys and disposes, doesn't it?'

'It does, exactly.'

'But we can't give a soldier an order 'destroy and dispose.' It's too long. The blighter could have ducked behind a rock by then.'

'True,' the Scientist said. 'We need a new word. How about DESTROPOSE'?'

'No.'

'No?'

'Not really. It sounds like a brand name. I can't ever see myself giving shouting an order – 'Destropose that man.''

'All right then,' rejoined the Scientist. 'How about 'DESTRUCTIFY'?'

'There's nothing about disposal in it.'

They fell silent for a few moments.

'Eureka!' the Scientist shouted. 'DESTRUCTIPOSE.'

'Yes. That's better. Bit long. Could pronounce it 'STRUCTIPOSE.'

'And spell it with a K instead of a C.'

'Better still.' The Brigadier shouted, 'DESTRUKTIPOSE! 'STRUKTIPOSE!' He fell silent, imagined himself back on the battlefield, and barked, 'Officer, 'struktipose that man!' He glanced at his watch, waited for five seconds and said, 'Well done, Officer.'

Foreknowledge of Jed's supposed intention would certainly have prevented the shock and tears that ensued. His fiancée was beside herself, fully convinced that he'd met with an accident or been kidnapped by her parents. She was relieved to find his suit neatly laid out. At least there was not another woman. All his effects were still intact. It didn't appear he'd planned to abscond.

'Did he have his wallet with him last night?' her mother asked.

'Of course.'

'And the tickets for the hotel?'

'I think so.'

'To put your mind at rest, my dear,' Mother said to daughter, 'I'll phone through to Bournemouth to see if he's checked in.'

Mother was convinced that Jed wouldn't waste expensive hotel reservations, certainly not at that hotel in Bournemouth she'd insisted was ideal for a honeymoon. He would either use them with someone else or get a refund. She wasn't altogether surprised he'd not turned up for the wedding, but when the hotel confirmed it had received no communication then she, too, began to think Jed might have had an accident.

She escorted his two friends to the police station where they reluctantly gave a full account of the incident. The Sergeant, on hearing of the blinding flash of light, immediately realised Jed had been the victim of Hoddinott's invention.

'By chance,' he said casually, 'do you know a man by the name of …' he remembered the confusion of names, but neither of the names themselves. He compromised. 'Hardiknot?'

'No. Why?

'Just a possibility. Something we're working on.'

He took down all the information, promising to let them know as soon as possible, explaining that an awful lot of people did seem to go missing these days and there was very little that could be done, what with the increase in real crime, though, of course, the police did their best.

'I'm sure you do,' said Mother. 'We really are grateful to you,' she added popping a coin in the collection box.

The Sergeant smiled and phoned the Superintendent, who passed the information to the Brigadier. The news that the gun worked successfully on human beings was received with great delight.

At the meeting of the Inner Cabinet Security Committee the Defence Minister arrived early and sat down in his usual seat, to the right hand of the Prime Minister's chair. The papers were in order, exhaustive reports and endless figures. He had prepared his speech thoroughly and rehearsed it mentally a dozen times. One by one the other Ministers came in. The Minister for Technology – 'Yes,' thought Defence, 'he's safe.' Any new scientific development was welcome to Lord Overlord. The Minister of Health was safe – so long as the birth rate exceeded the death rate the nation was judged to be healthy. And as it did so at the moment the healthy nation needed protection even if that meant possible deaths. Transport was safe, too. He was forever telling the world 'Take Radar, for instance. No war. No technology.' The Foreign Secretary and Overseas Development came in together.

'Mmm,' thought Defence, 'the safest and the shakiest.'

The Prime Minister was late as usual.

'The prerogative of royalty,' quipped the Lord Chancellor, a strict disciplinarian and a much-loved after-dinner speaker. The remark always raised a laugh either from those, among them the Lord Chancellor himself, who thought a little blue blood desirable in the veins of the Chief Minister of the Crown, or from those who thought the Prime Minister's high-handedness an undesirable trait in a democratically-elected Tribune of the People.

'Gentlemen,' said the Prime Minister entering briskly, 'do not let us delay any longer.'

The issue of the weapon was second to last on the agenda. Overseas Development said it should have priority. It was put to a vote and voted down. Almost an hour passed and other issues were hotly debated. Was the new uniform in the recruiting poster for policewomen too provocative? Should the heads of famous people be allowed to appear alongside the Queen on commemorative coins? Surely the line had to be drawn at Churchill and Shakespeare? With Robert Burns as a sop to Scottish Nationalism? But what about Welsh Nationalism? What about it indeed? Were there any famous Welsh people – apart, of course, from the Prince of Wales? By the time the weapons issue came up most Ministers were exhausted – except Defence who had barely said two words, and then only 'Hear! Hear!'

His turn now came. He stood up and quite consciously disarranged his papers so everyone could see the reports and tables of figures marked 'Confidential.'

'Human nature is a funny thing,' he began, pausing to give the Foreign Secretary time to nod his agreement. 'Killing in wartime may be a very wrong, but necessary act. But human interest is not so much fascinated by the fact that a man is killed as how he is killed. The method of killing is what interests us. The more horrific, the more fascinating. Some people say hanging is barbaric. They would rather a lethal injection or the electric chair, but they still believe in capital punishment. It is the method they object to, not the aim. Some people say fox-hunting is cruel and would instead set traps so the foxes die of starvation, or gnaw off their paws. These people agree that foxes should be kept in check. It is the method of doing so they feel strongly about. It's the same with religion. There have been crueller deaths than the Crucifixion. Wars and massacres have made this one death seem insignificant. It's the horror of the Cross – that particular method of execution – that retains the fascination.

'Surely the real point is not how we kill but that we kill. Some soldiers cut off the heads of their victims and stick them on poles. We call this depravity, but the real depravity is the killing. Cannibals kill and then eat their victims; we call this barbarity. Killing is the real crime, mutilation after death is an irrelevance, distasteful, yes, but not the real crime. Was there ever a more stupid story than that of Antigone who wanted a dead body given a decent funeral, but thought of no sort of revenge on the people who'd killed it? "Let the dead bury the dead." The method of killing is not the point. It is whether killing has to take place. It sometimes, unfortunately, does. It is my job as Minister of Defence to ensure we are equipped to do this should it be necessary – which we all hope it won't. Now – let us be reasonable – this new weapon kills, and disposes, by a new method. And none too pleasant. But the fact remains that the act of killing, not the method, is the point of issue and it is that – when and if the need arises – that we should try and resolve. Meanwhile we cannot afford to be without any weapon, the international situation being what it is.'

He arranged his papers in order again, implying that further evidence was available in the unlikely event of it being requested. He then sat down. The Foreign Secretary applauded. He bent over to Defence.

'Did you say you were a barrister before coming to Parliament?'

'No.'

'You could well have been. Some fine legal distinctions there.'

'But,' Overseas Development protested, 'this weapon disposes of the evidence. No-one will ever know there's been a crime.'

'True,' retorted Defence. 'That's why I have ensured by the strictest and most stringent regulations that this weapon is kept secret, and in the hands of only those who can be trusted to use it.'

'You're making this a top secret matter?'

'Of course,' snapped Defence and tidied his papers still further so that not a chink of lettering could be seen, 'and for the very reason you gave.' He paused and added pointedly. 'Think if the … underworld stumbled on it.'

'Horrific,' muttered the Home Secretary. 'We'd need more policewomen then.'

'Or foreign powers. Double agents,' the Foreign Secretary said.

'Or the Opposition,' quipped the Lord Chancellor, who thought the Defence Minister's legal distinctions facile.

'The situation is unthinkable,' Defence clinched. 'It is top secret. No discussions whatsoever. Is that not so?'

This question was addressed to no-one in particular but everyone assumed after looking at each other's glum faces that Higher Authority in the person of the Prime Minister was expected to reply. As it was the Prime Minister, serene of countenance, stood up and remarked –

'I'm glad this issue came near the end of the agenda. You'll all be able to go away with the thought of Top Secrecy uppermost. Indeed I think the last item can safely be dropped.'

There was general agreement. Overseas Development looked peeved. In the secret vote on whether the weapons issue should have priority the Premier had obviously voted against him. They filed out. The Prime Minister beckoned Defence over to the window.

'You handled that very well. Bye-the-bye, what did the Foreign Secretary say to you?'

'He said he thought my argument was full of fine legal distinctions.'

'So it was. So it was. So he's interested in Law, is he?' queried the Premier. 'That's interesting. In the forthcoming reshuffle we could make him Lord Chancellor. We do so need a change at the – er – Foreign Office.'

'Come in,' the Minister of Defence said, and in came the Brigadier, Chief of Secret Research. 'Ah, Brigadier. What can I do for you?'

The Brigadier was grim-faced. He carried no brief-case, pouch or clip-board, and was in civilian clothes, but his looks betrayed he was armed for battle.

'It's about the Destruktopositer.'

'There's been no hitch or complication, has there?'

'No, there hasn't.'

'Well, then, what's the trouble?'

'I feel that we must tell the Chief of Army Personnel.'

It had been difficult for the Brigadier to bring himself to say this. He didn't want the information to go out of his department, but he felt his duty to the Army as a whole demanded it.

'Oh no,' the Minister retorted. 'The matter must go no further than you, Chief of Research.'

'I feel it must.'

The Minister smiled slightly. What was he hearing? Insubordination? He was angered and intrigued.

'Why, pray?'

'For the sake of the men.'

'What men?'

'The fighting men.'

'Quite what have the fighting men to do with the Destrukitiposiwosi – whatever it is? They mustn't know about it. Surely this is clear?'

'Of course. Unless they have to use it.'

'We'll sort that one out when we come to it. I've thought about it, of course. It is a problem, I admit, but one for when the war is actually on.'

'No,' the Brigadier replied. 'That's not the issue. What I want to know is this.' He jabbed his forefinger on the Minister's desk, making little dents in the leather covering. 'How are we going to decorate the men?'

'Decorate them? Put them in a special uniform, do you mean?' The Minister easily tired of sub-committees, commissions, honours and all the appurtenances of bureaucracy. And now a suggestion for a special regiment – decorated!

'I don't mean that,' the Brigadier protested. 'A fighting man in my day was promoted partly on the number of enemy casualties he caused. This new weapon will dispose of the bodies. We won't know who to promote. Hadn't thought of that, had you? I've racked my brains to find a solution. But it's beyond me. I must refer it to the Chief of Personnel.'

The Minister had not thought of it either, and he let the Brigadier continue in order to give himself time to think.

'The whole basis,' the Brigadier went on, 'of promotion by merit will be undermined. If the man in the field cannot show evidence of his skill and expect due recognition what incentive will he have? He'll need special training – admittedly, as you say, after the conflict has begun – but will they get any recognition? Special recognition?'

'What do you mean special recognition?'

'A special order – the Order of Destruktiposifaction.'

'Oh, don't be such a fool,' the Minister snapped. 'The George Cross covers everything.'

'It's not purely military, sir.'

'Well, the Victoria Cross then. Whatever. What does it matter anyway?'

He looked at the Brigadier. It obviously mattered a lot to him.

'Now. No. Perhaps I was a bit hasty there. Put it like this, Brigadier. The question doesn't arise until a war breaks out. The weapon wouldn't be issued to everyone. We're not going to mass produce it. Indeed' – a saving thought crossed his mind – 'it wouldn't be issued at all. For it would only be used against a special victim – the enemy leader or someone, the Chief of Staff, someone important – someone who is an undeniable risk. On the field the men would use guns as usual. The new weapon could be used to dispose of the dead bodies. Do you see? It's their commander or someone we want to polish off and we'd want to do that fully – in one go – without leaving any evidence. It would be a special mission, quite separate from the fighting men's tasks. So you see the question of promotion doesn't arise, does it, Brigadier? And the matter won't need to go to the Chief of Personnel, will it?'

'I see, well, if that's the case then …' He trailed off, much mollified.

'And of course,' the Minister took over, 'the special mission itself would be entrusted to someone who could not expect to be promoted, as he will be already of the highest rung.'

'The highest rung, Minister? You mean the Chief of … Me?' The Brigadier was greatly flattered. It had been many years since he had seen active service.

'Not necessarily you, Brigadier. An absolute Chief would be too valuable, but one of your deputies perhaps.'

'If the mission was of sufficient importance I would be only too …'

'I know, Brigadier, but let's hope it doesn't come to that. Let's hope there never is a war. After all,' he said, making an expansive gesture and levelling the dents in his desk leather, 'it is our business to prevent war.'

'Indeed, yes,' the Brigadier replied, pleased that the secret was to be kept in his department, and that the prospect of future military glory might come his way.

The Prime Minister had summoned the Lord Chancellor, and the Lord Chancellor was late. He could not but drag his feet, being overcome with premonition. As he walked through St James's Park he noted the various species of duck that swam on the lake. He scored the gravel with the tip of his umbrella, much as Euclid must have made his marks in the sand, but whereas Euclid was pursuing a theory his Lordship was pursuing nothing. Indeed he was lost in a mental maze and no graphologist could have deciphered the marks he left.

He knew he was no favourite of the Prime Minister and had long anticipated the call which would mean his enforced retirement. He couldn't rely on any of his colleagues for support. They belittled him for his aristocratic ways, and for short called the Office of Lord Chancellor, L.C., and himself Elsie. He tried to re-establish his image by advocating tough measures against law-breakers, and by introducing more punitive laws. Personally he didn't object to returning to the back benches of the Upper House. He had a pleasant country mansion, which could boast more species of duck on its lake than could St James's Park, but then if being an altogether larger lake and His Lordship being a past President of the Wildfowl Trust, this was hardly surprising. What he did object to was the thought that his replacement would undoubtedly be a dynamic, go-ahead know-all – probably elevated from the back-benches of the Lower House – who would introduce all the changes, so long, and by and large so successfully, resisted.

He entered the Cabinet Room and smiled apologetically to its only other occupant.

'I have a very unpleasant duty to perform,' began the Prime Minister. 'I have to request you to do as I say.' He paced the room, trying to keep upright while dragging down the lapels of his jacket. 'And keep what I say a secret – though you won't like it.'

Yes, thought the Lord Chancellor, I'm sure I won't.

'In the interest of national security you must agree to what I say.'

National security? Was the Lord Chancellor a danger to the state?

'The situation is this …'

Here we go, thought His Lordship – lengthy explanations, justifications, excuses.

'A new and deadly weapon has been invented which, at all costs, must remain secret. The Cabinet has been sworn to secrecy. We discussed it last week as you will recall. The inventor of this weapon is a former sewage disposer who got the idea from the Scientific Branch of his works, just before retiring. His name is Hardiknot – or is it Hardinoff. I forget. Hardenoff, I think. Sounds foreign to me. Anyway, he's now in jail for using the weapon against a trespasser. He's threatening quite vehemently, to expose this secret to the world – once he's freed. The man's a fool to be sure, and the police say he could be certified insane. Few people are likely to listen to him, but we can't take any risks. If he goes on trial for manslaughter he may get five years, or, at the most, seven. He's only sixty-five and could well survive prison and pass the information to an enemy power. Indeed in prison he could pass it on to other criminals. There's no way of silencing him if the case goes through the Courts. He must be kept in solitary confinement until he dies. And you, as Lord Chancellor, must agree that this is a case where normal legal procedures should be suspended in the interests of national security. The man, in effect, is to be held without trial as a political prisoner. Under the terms of the Secrets Act a government is empowered, in exceptional circumstances, to do this – but as head of the Legal Establishment in this country your sanction is required.'

The Lord Chancellor was taken aback – he knew about the weapon but not the predicament of the inventor. He was surprised that the Prime Minister was asking permission to do something.

'Political prisoner, Premier?'

'True, contrary to all this country, the Law and especially our Party has stood for. But it is a necessity. There is a worse option. That might happen in other countries. This man, Hardenoff, is incorrigible and couldn't be trusted with his freedom even if he promised to remain silent.'

'My dear Premier, off-hand I can think of no precedent.'

'Not in this country, no. There is none. Imprisonment during wartime. But without trial, without possible remission, merely for having invented a piece of equipment that potentially, as I understand it, could be of great use to conservation – who must of necessity be kept in jail for defence reasons – a well-meaning man this er – Hardenoff, no doubt, yes – no, there is no precedent for this. Not in this country. Nor ...' he trailed off rather, incoherently.

'But the Law does operate on precedents and no new one can be established save through Parliament or the Courts.'

'I am aware of this.'

'And you still ask me to waive this man's claim to a fair hearing?'

'In the interests of security, yes. Parliament and the Courts must be by-passed. The Inner Cabinet knows about the weapon. They've been sworn to secrecy. They do not know about its inventor. In their ignorance they attribute the invention to the Defence Ministry. Only seven people know of the true inventor – myself, three policemen, the Chief of Army Secret Research and his Scientific Adviser, the Minister of Defence – and Hardenoff, of course. No-one else must know. Seven is too many. In telling you, my dear fellow, I have increased the number, but unless I thought you thoroughly trustworthy and reliable I would not, of course, have done so. You realise this?'

The Lord Chancellor nodded.

'Now having told you, with your permission, the necessary arrangements must be made. They are, I think you will agree, rather ingenious. The three policemen – a Station Sergeant, a Station Superintendent and a detective – will be transferred to the police section of the Ministry of Defence to act as warders to Hardenoff, each on eight hour shifts, thus making them Hardenoff's prisoners as much as he theirs. That disposes of them rather effectively. Hardenoff himself must – assuming he is ever missed, and I understand he led a sheltered life – be added to the list of missing persons. The two public servants have permanent posts. The Chief of Research is totally reliable and, according to the Minister of Defence, willing to do anything. The Scientific Adviser is happy experimenting regardless of result. They're safe enough.

'Thus we are left with three Ministers. Defence is a difficulty; he should by rights go the Foreign Office but this would mean a new Minister of Defence and the extension of our secret. I have therefore decided that the Foreign Secretary be elevated to the peerage and made Minister without Portfolio – I shall keep him amused with various assignments, heading investigations, trouble shooting – that sort of thing. And the Foreign Office itself will be incorporated into the Ministry of Defence. In this way foreign policy is made subservient to defence. National security is thus furthered. With your support I shall remain Prime Minister and you, my Lord, must remain Lord Chancellor for the duration of your or Hardenoff's life.'

'I am guaranteed my position for life?' the Lord Chancellor gasped.

'Just so.'

'But,' the Lord Chancellor queried, thinking the arrangements just a little too simple, 'what about elections? I know they're not for four years ...'

'Elections?' laughed the Minister of Defence, breezing in. 'No need to worry. Sort that one out when we come to it, eh?'

'You're late, my dear fellow,' the Prime Minister said. 'I've just finished telling his Lordship about the weapons affair.'

'Indeed, yes. Defence of the realm determines foreign policy and sometimes internal policy, too. I hope you've agreed to the Prime Minister's plans. They're rather neat, aren't they?'

The Lord Chancellor bowed his head. 'I see I must agree. We are all Hardenov's prisoners. We have no room for manoeuvre.'

'Yes, I suppose you could look at it that way.'

'Prisoners of technology and progress. Do you not think, Premier, that your championship of these things may have precipitated this situation?'

'No, it was Hadenoff, on his own, who invented this machine.'

'With the co-operation of the Scientific Branch of his – sewage works, did you not say?'

'Not co-operation, no. He was trained by them. He used his training independently after his retirement.'

The Lord Chancellor shrugged. 'But we are prisoners of this man, as he is of us.'

'Yes, we are guaranteed our positions and the burdens they involve, above all the burden of secrecy. As you say, our positions are our prisons. But let's not be too pessimistic? Come! Come!'

'Yes, let's forget Hadenoff,' the Minister of Defence said. 'I've had enough of Hadenoff.'

The interview ended. A Triumvirate of Prime Minister, Lord Chancellor and Minister of Defence had been agreed. Law,

Discipline, Leadership. 'Law and Order' the election slogan that had swept the Party to victory.

The Prime Minister looked out the window and saw the Lord Chancellor and the Minister of Defence walking across Horse Guards Parade.

'So glad his Lordship felt able to agree. Otherwise Defence would have insisted on using the weapon against its inventor. Couldn't have lived with that.'

He walked across the room, passed the mirror and nodded to himself. He turned and paced back to the window. No-one was in sight. He glanced up to the sky for strength and absolution.

Coping

Coping

"Of course, you realise certain men never – really – marry."

Mrs Clyne couldn't take kindly to this.

She accepted readily enough that for the last few months her marriage had been incomplete. She didn't accept, however, that it had never been a success. It had been. A few months could never erase the many years of happiness. She had experienced the joys and tribulations of raising a child. She was struck by the worthwhileness of it all.

She wasn't going to wish it all away. Or say she'd been wrong to marry in the first place. Nor was she prepared to accept the over-indulgent sympathy of outsiders who assumed she'd always been unhappy and had never really known what 'true marriage is all about'.

"They're so wedded to their job, you see."

Of course, a Marriage Guidance Counsellor would think that!

Mrs Clyne had told him so when she began the consultations. She'd told him intentionally in order to weigh the evidence in her favour. There was something glib and naïve in the way it was now being repeated to her as if it was his original insight.

Who was this Counsellor anyway?

"This is particularly true of service life, which is so different to civilian life."

That was true.

Life in the Forces was exciting. The long absences did make the heart grow fonder. You got to know the husband from short, passionate bursts of contact and could reflect on these during the long separations. The erratic hours, and the continual moving from one base to another, held so much more expectation and demanded so much more resourcefulness than a staid, suburban civilian marriage. She was forever finding herself tested by changes of location and face – but she'd coped. And had managed to provide homes which were adequate to bring up her daughter and entertain her husband's service colleagues.

That was important. She feared the accusation of not being able to cope, of being incompetent. To be incompetent in a society that competed was, according to the military mind of her husband, like being a non-combattant.

"All service personnel are subjected to extreme pressures, and their marriages are very susceptible to break-up."

Then why had she known so many happy marriages?

True, she'd never known a service couple for any length of time – one never did – but she'd met couples who'd been together for decades. There may have been infidelities, but they were always denied in terms that emphasised some indissoluble link between marital and martial loyalty. Still, she had known of some undeniably genuine love-matches, and until recently thought her own marriage was one of them.

In truth – and she'd never told this to the Counsellor – she felt that the less attention her husband paid to his job the more likelihood there was of disagreement. Almost for something to say she'd complained to Xavier of the difficulties of being continually on the move, of the bad effect on the girl's schooling, of how a girl needed stability and an understanding, ever-present father. Xavier, to her surprise, had agreed.

'I'll be grounded soon enough,' he had said. 'I may as well choose the timing myself.'

He was transferred to an administrative section in Whitehall. He worked regular hours and wore civilian clothes. For the first time since their marriage they'd been able to settle in a home of their own.

"The nature of the job is such that neither party can see the nature of true marriage."

That actually applied more to Xavier's new job.

She didn't know exactly what his new job entailed. In active service he'd been full of himself, telling her everything, bragging and boasting. Now, he never gave much away. She never met any of his colleagues. He was forever making remarks at the expense of this or that minority or ethnic group. She supposed his job was some sort of internal intelligence work. She laughed. He was not up in the air any longer, but did something equally nebulous. Well, he seemed to enjoy it, whatever it was. And, as he said, he had coped.

It posed her difficulties, though. She saw much more of Xavier than ever before. He ceased to be continually in her mind the more he was almost continually in her presence. During his long absences abroad she had worried for his safety, had a pride in the vital dashing job she imagined he was doing, lapped up the sympathy from friends who admired her for living under the shadow of premature widowhood. These were compensations. Perhaps it had been a consolation to think of her husband's death. Now the more remote the possibility the more she relished the prospect.

She even hinted to Xavier he might like to return to a more active branch of the Service. He refused, saying, 'I'd never be reinstated. Anyway, it's nice to have a home of one's own, instead of defending other people's.' He pointed out that the transfer had been requested on the grounds his marriage was endangered by his frequent absences. He could hardly go back on that.

And she could hardly say she'd been wrong – and that now the real danger to the marriage was his continual presence.

And she could hardly mention any of this to the Marriage Guidance Counsellor who was continuing to extol the joys of the breakfast table.

"Marriage, you see, is a two-way process."

Oh, yes! Quite. No doubt.

What she missed was the occasional excitement – the parties in the mess, decked out with chandeliers, the food, the music and dancing, the sense of occasion. True, the talk was limited. No religion, no politics. That, in effect, left only one subject, an inexhaustible one – promotion.

She missed the free time as well. On the camp she could get away just by refusing to attend yet another function. The whole quarters would empty. There'd be distant sounds of merriment, and she could collect her thoughts, day-dream, or just stare over the flat, desolate expanse of the airfield runways.

Her new home was a semi-detached in suburbia, not quite as peaceful as expected. The moment she opened the door or windows she was greeted by an antiphon of hoovers, different radio stations, gossip meant to be overheard, delivery vans screeching to a halt, children shouting, dogs barking, and a neighbour's pet mynah bird giving wolf whistles to every passer-by.

After years of transient friendships on the camp she found it difficult to hit it off with her new and ever-present neighbours. She needed to mix with them to get out of Xavier's way. She discovered in baby-sitting a way of being regarded as a 'decent sort' without having to mingle in a social event. Much of her time was now spent in the quiet of other people's homes.

"The initial bond of attraction – and we must be mature enough to admit that it is usually physical – cannot be sustained without the underpinning of lesser daily tasks. Domesticity. Familiarity. Shared experiences. Division of roles. All these have to be worked at. For they come less naturally than the original attraction."

So what had been the original attraction?

It was astute of the Counsellor to mention this. Only recently she felt moved to go through her husband's clothes, trying to recall the memorable occasions he'd worn them. She'd got no further than his Air Force uniform – which he now never wore, and probably couldn't get into.

Had this piece of blue cloth, camouflaged the colour of the skies, really lured her to marry Xavier? Did she love men in uniform? There was something no-nonsense about them. They presented in one go, beliefs and commitments. You knew where you stood with them. You accepted them and did not challenge them. True, they were unsubtle, school uniforms writ large. One grew out of them, often for the same reasons one had been attracted to them. But there was an initial impact. She could never mentally undress a man in uniform – that was part of the fascination. He would have to do it himself, when he thought fit – and that was part of his strength.

The awful fact now was that though Xavier never wore his uniform he still behaved as if he was wearing it. Since being grounded, and presumably having fewer underlings to boss around, he'd grown progressively more military with her. Even in bed he grunted his orders as if he were on manoeuvres. He'd kiss her neck on one side, then on the other side with the injunction "Left! Right!' – then 'Left! Right!' for her shoulders. He'd move down a little further and order 'Hands up!' And kiss her just below the left armpit – which did nothing for her – and move slowly down to the left breast and end with a quick bite on the nipple as if planting a flag on a newly-scaled mountain. And, then, just as she was getting a bit worked up, he'd leave the left side and go

103

to the right armpit. Everything was dealt with methodically, but not in a sequence of rising passion. Below the breasts the kissing stopped, and his fingers started running down her stomach like a spider running backwards. Then he'd run his fingers from the far side of the bed and suddenly parachute onto her stomach. He did this several times in succession like a series of exits from the trenches. With each sortie his fingers got nearer the target area. Just outside, they stopped; and ten soldiers helped in the cannon reinforcement. A few seconds of battery and he'd gasp, 'Enemy destroyed, sir!' And the enemy's condition was in no way tended before an inordinately hasty retreat.

It was the same every night. Years ago it had excited her. She'd played along. It was acceptable when coupled with the passion she genuinely felt when he returned after months posted away. Nowadays, she felt under enemy occupation.

She put the uniform back in the wardrobe. What difference was there between this uniform – symbol of one way of life and beliefs – and any other passing fashion? Didn't anoraks and jeans and spiky cropped hair also presuppose life-styles, outlooks, attitudes? Wasn't the blue of Xavier's uniform almost the same as that of denim? She could go for that as well. She might even find a certain delight in embracing the sort of 'scum' and 'human detritus' her husband so condemned.

"There must be give. And there must be take. Ideally there should in every action be a combination of the two. Of give – and take!"

Christ! What drivel!

Who was this Counsellor, anyway? Younger than herself and giving her advice. She looked at him closely. He distantly resembled her brother, Royston – except that her brother had more sense. And could give better advice. Perhaps she could arrange to see him, perhaps tell him of her troubles.

She'd lost contact recently. Royston and Xavier did not hit it off, which she put down to a clash of military and artistic temperaments. It hadn't mattered previously. She'd been able to see Royston when Xavier was abroad. It was more difficult now.

She found Royston somewhat unapproachable. She shared few of his tastes and interests, and felt less educated and slightly inferior to him. She tried to compensate by stressing her achievement in creating a family. When Royston snorted and pointed out that this was not unique, that only uncreative people felt the need to have children, she would counter and say – Yes, it was unique. Only she could treat her child as an 'individual' and know her special needs and tend to them. No-one else could do that. And who knows? The girl might grow up to be a great artist, not just appreciating art – being artistic – but actually performing it, even creating it. This always trumped Royston.

"A two-way process! The more so when blessed with the appearance of a child. A third force, not divisive but cementing the union."

Would that were true!

In fact Xavier showed less interest in little Veronica's development than Royston did. Previously on the air-bases the girl had attended special schools and spent the rest of the day at home. She was under more pressure now. Royston appreciated that she needed extra support. He treated her like a grown-up and helped with her homework, even tested her. He was eager she benefit from her new environment, and offered to show her round places of interest. But Xavier's dislike of him precluded that happening.

The last time Royston had visited it was actually Veronica who caused the embarrassment. Mrs Clyne had said, 'When Uncle Roy comes ask him to test you.'

In the event the testing took a different form. Royston arrived with a large box of chocolates. Veronica, who was playing at the far end of the garden, heard the rustle of wrapping paper and bounded up on her spindly legs.

'Hello, Uncle Roy. Oh, Mummy. Look! Chocolates! Will you test me?'

'Test you?'

'Yes. You know. We always play at testing when we have chocolates.'

'Do we, dear?'

'Yes, Mummy. Go on.'

'Oh, alright. Which one is round and has a gold wrapper?'

'With a squiggly bit on top?'

'Yes.'

'That's easy. That's coffee cream.'

'Right.'

'Can I have it?'

'Here you are then.'

'Now you test me, Uncle Roy.'

'Well, let's see. Which one has no wrapper and is diamond-shaped?'

'Chocolate toffee.'

'Well done. Here you are. You have got a good memory, haven't you?'

'Yes, and my teacher says I'm doing very well, too. Doesn't he, Mummy?'

'Yes, dear.'

'Can I have one more please?'

'You haven't eaten that one already, have you? You're supposed to chew toffees.'

'Oh, PLEASE, Mummy. Test me.'

'You've had two.'

'Oh, let her have another one,' laughed Royston. 'Test her again,' he added emphasising the word test.

'Must I? Oh, alright. Which one has no wrapper and three little lumps?'

'Hazlenut.'

'Correct. Here you are. Open wide and I'll pop it in.'

'Oh, Mummy. You've given me the ginger one.'

'Oh, have I, darling?'

'It's horrid. Urgh!'

'What a silly mistake. You know I didn't mean it. You should look what you put in your mouth.'

'But you put it in.'

'So I did. So I did.'

Mrs Clyne laughed at the recollection. Serve the silly little girl right. She may be my daughter but ...

But what had Royston really thought? She couldn't know. She'd invite him down. Perhaps he could bring some of his college friends, some of the ones that Xavier criticised so readily.

I might even tell him about some of my troubles. After all he is my brother. And blood is thicker than Marriage Guidance Counsellor's dribble.

"Once this happy union has been achieved one realises that it is the prime aim of humankind. The stability and security of the basic unit is the determining factor in all decisions. Even work and ambition become secondary."

Was there, alas, something in this?

Yes. She had security. She was given plenty of money. There was no real need for her to work. Part-time work mildly attracted her, more as charity than for remuneration, some cut-above, slightly tasteful job that needed little training but sounded worthy. Perhaps working in a bookshop or library, or teaching English to foreigners. She might meet interesting people – it might be a means to an end. Yet equally it might be further time-filling, with no real output. The impetus was not really there. Nor the imperative.

There was no real necessity for her to go outside the front door. Xavier never did once he was home. He never did any jobs around the house. He hired workmen, decorators, window cleaners. He had the garden paved and bricked and the plants containerised. It was a model town garden and just needed sweeping once a week. He expected her to follow his example and have as much as possible done and delivered, leaving only the fresh food to buy, and the evening meal to prepare. There was nothing she could reasonably complain about in this arrangement. If she protested Xavier would have replied – as she had no doubt all the outside world would have replied – 'She's got a home, security, money, a child, and everything done for her. What more does the silly bitch want?'

"All immature longings, personal expression, so-called creativity, disappear in the face of the willingly-chosen imperative of life."

If that ever were true, it was fast ceasing to be so.

She looked with more than passing interest at the delivery men, the milkman and the postman. But it was the laundryman she thought of most, and not just while she was putting the clean linen on the bed and smoothing out the wrinkles. How could one feel guilty when thinking about a man who ran a laundry? He must know all about the tell-tale stains of love. His job was to wash them away, a kind of absolution, almost a confession. She was even surprised to find herself casting an appreciative eye on the paperboy, who in a matter of months had shot up from being a shy, gangling wisp to a confident, clothes-conscious youth.

She planned her day by their arrival. She tried to imagine their lives. She knew nothing would 'happen' and so what if it did? It would only be a modern variant of sex with the servants. Sometimes she fantasised about the men who didn't merely deliver goods but actually came into the house. Not the quick visits of meter-readers, nor even of plumbers and decorators, but of lodgers.

And lodgers were a possibility given the size of the house. She'd have some advantage over them – not so much a hold, as a legitimate excuse to be pleasant to anyone on her territory.

She felt similarly about foreigners and new residents. They might be grateful in their new surroundings for a friendly face, discreet advice or help with filling forms. They'd be thankful she showed no objection to their presence. It would give her a feeling of virtue, mission even. She had a certain expectation of them, if only in the way they might behave to her.

She spent hours shopping, trailing round market stalls and ethnic food shops, toying with exotic items she did not really know what to do with. She read the labels, smiled at the assistants and asked what she believed were telling questions. She became a regular at the shops where the assistants were the most receptive and talkative. She might – helpfully she thought – correct their English, and expect them to thank her for it. She didn't often buy much on the first visit, but when she got home she'd regret not having bought a certain item she'd toyed with. She often made a second visit, and stocked up in excess.

But whenever she tried out foreign meals Xavier picked at the food, grunted he preferred plain English cooking – nourishing stews, wholesome joints, filling puddings, fry-ups even.

She couldn't even persuade him to go out to a restaurant.

'There's a new Malaysian Restaurant opened in the High Street. It's supposed to be very good. Can we try it?'

The answer was always 'We'll see' or 'Possibly' or 'I spent three months over there, if you remember.'

Everything about that man was getting so predictable. When he was in the Air Force proper he came back changed by each assignment, as if the culture of the place had rubbed off on him. He brought back mementoes – and told her of different ways of life and strange goings-on. Perhaps each time she had – had she? – imagined him as a foreigner telling her about his own land.

More fool her if she had! She didn't doubt now that many of his tales were hearsay picked up from the Senior Officers he'd been trying to imitate. Even the mementoes he'd bought back, and which then seemed so unusual, were now readily available, imported en masse, some even made locally.

What she'd seen as vital and dashing in him she now saw as repressive. But she was finding her voice. Only last week they'd been looking at television together. The News Broadcast featured the anniversary celebrations of an Independence Day.

'Forty years ago we were shooting those bastards. Now look at them jumping up and down!'

She replied – to her own and Xavier's surprise – 'Good luck to them. Why shouldn't they rule themselves?'

"We need dependence to prevent ourselves lying fallow. Independence is alright in theory. But it is lonely and arid and is not the soil in which anything can grow."

Yes, she was lying fallow. But not for the reasons given.

She wanted someone to depend on and turn to if she were to make the break with Xavier. She needed to be able to say 'I'm in love' which sounded far more convincing than 'I'm fed up.' It took her into a far more authoritative realm of argument, a definite alternative is always better than a vague complaint.

But who could help her to make the break? A passing stranger would do. A student just beginning to fend for himself, not coping too well, who might well be responsive to an older woman's attentions. A foreigner or a new resident, confused, looking for guidance, a rock to cling to before finding his own feet. Perhaps one of Royston's friends? Did it matter exactly who? Someone to help make the break. Afterwards, if she felt the need, she could look for some permanent set-up. The long term was secondary.

It must happen soon. If left any longer Veronica would lose her gaucheness and shoot up as quickly as the paperboy had done. And then the men would be making eyes at her. Mother and daughter as rivals? No, that mustn't happen! It must be soon. But who would the man be? What would he be like?

She looked intently at the Counsellor as he continued his advice.

"The greatest joy and strength in life comes from the open yet complete union of the basic unit of society."

Was he really so bad, this Counsellor? Were there possibilities? Would he answer her questions as well as giving advice? She'd been silent too long.

'Excuse me. May I ask you a question?'

'In the normal course of consultation that would not be allowable. However. Just this once. If you wish. I suppose.'

'Are you married?'

'Thank you so much for asking that. Only last week – after several years of acquaintance – a very wonderful woman agreed to become my fiancée.'

'I see. I think.'

The Heights

The Heights

'There'll be a few extra houses this year,' the supervisor said.

It was the second year that I had done the Christmas mail, and I'd been given the same round, on the far side of the town. They always give you a round away from where you live, presumably so you don't get to know your neighbours' business or drop in for a chat.

'About six more houses. You don't mind?'

I was grateful. I hadn't been able to get any work since the previous Christmas.

'That's good. The regular postmen aren't keen on it.'

'I see.'

'It's called Spratt's Enclave. Ever heard of it?'

I shrugged.

'It's a new development. Posh. Between the main road and the disused railway line.'

'I see.'

The area between the main road and the old railway line? No, I hadn't heard of it by that name. When we played there as children we'd always called it – the woods.

I picked up the mail-bag and set out. I could see why the regular postmen were glad to offload this part of the round. It wasn't a particularly neighbourly area. I was used to delivery boxes and entry phones like the ones we have in our block of flats; or even terraced houses where you could nip over fences and walls from one house to another. But here, there wasn't even a communal pillar box at the main access point from the road.

Each house in the Enclave was along a winding path; one on the level, one in a dip, another discreetly angled overlooking the hillside; all parceled out, wrapped up, individually addressed, the Dene, the Dell, the Hollow, the Heights. Each had kept a screen of the original woodland trees, supplemented with mature transplants of laburnum, copper beech, flowering cherry and magnolia. I wasn't sure if they failed to root properly or were at their worst in the winter. Years ago in our quieter moments, between evicting rival gangs, we'd gone in for identifying all the woodland plants.

There was no evidence of recent building work, no piles of bricks or sand. There were plenty of log piles, outside back doors and sheds. It had a woodman's cottage feel about it. And a dank, fungal smell. And sinister, wasn't it, the way the houses had mushroomed overnight behind their screen of trees?

Most of our old getaway paths had been re-routed. The clumps of bushes, overhung with creepers and briars, that we'd used as hide-outs, had been cleared or been thinned out. Many trees remained, including our principal look-out tree, at the very boundary of our former territory – the Sacred Piss Tree. It was here, as part of an unsworn brotherhood, we mingled our urine in mid-air. It was under this tree, when the brotherhood was betrayed, that we tried Julian and condemned him to eternal exile.

'If you ever come back,' said Bobby, who was much older that the rest of us, 'it'll be as Julienne garnish.'

We did not, at that time, understand the reference, but were suitably impressed. Bobby, who claimed to be a trainee chef, often made threats in terms of food. 'You know what's for lunch today, don't you?' he'd say grabbing our collars and snarling into our faces, 'Bollocks on toast.' Occasionally, he threatened to devil our kidneys or serve us up our own chopped liver. The meals offered were usually abdominal snacks, always on toast. He disappeared from our lives quite suddenly. His younger brother, mature for his years, said he'd found a niche in a prison canteen.

A shout from behind brought me up with a start.

'Give them to us.'

Four children, their scarves swathed round their necks like terrorists, swooped out from the trees.

'Give you what?' I snarled.

'Our letters.'

'How do I know you're from here?' I asked.

'Are you the new postman?'

'The other one knew who we were.'

'We liked him.'

'Where is he?'

'He's dead, isn't he?'

'You killed him and took his job.'

'I don't even think you're a postman.'

'Nor do I. Prove you're a postman.'

'Prove you're the children of the house,' I countered.

'I'll tell Mummy. She said someone nasty was coming,' said the oldest girl.

'Where's your ID and your uniform?'

I pointed between my coat buttons to my chest badge.

'You're not supposed to wear a coat over it.'

'I can't see all the gold round the edges,' said the eldest, importantly.

'That's what Daddy calls scrambled egg,' added the youngest.

'Postmen don't have that kind of uniform,' I said.

'I don't believe you. Take your coat off.'

'We want to see how much gold braid you've got.'

'Take it off.'

'Make him take his clothes off.'

'Make him take his clothes off,' they chorused, dancing around. They plucked at the mail bag. I was tempted to swing it round my head and hit out at them. I adjusted it so it strapped safely across my chest like a school satchel.

They ran off daring 'Catch me. Catch me.'

They all looked the same in their hooded coats, patterned scarves, mittens and hats with bobbles. Little brats! I hated them all.

They ran alongside me, peeping out the bushes and pretending to play hide and seek, and unexpectedly jumping in front of me shouting 'Boo!'

Don't think I'm going to join your feeble games. I played better ones when I was your age.

'Catch me! Catch me!' and they disappeared into the trees.

'Get lost!'

I particularly hated Robin, the youngest. But most of all I hated the oldest girl. She was bossy and breast-buddy, at the age when a welcome smile can lead into an accusation of attempted rape.

'Catch me,' she cried. 'Catch me.'

Fuck yourself.

Who was this family anyway? Unopened mail can be as revealing as raking through a dustbin. There were several mailing lists, three for books and one for compact discs. The rest were from financial institutions, half from abroad. They looked more formal than junk mail. I assumed the owner to be an international broker or . . .

'Catch us!' came a distant cry.

. . . and the father of those brats.

I turned the winding path to what had been our principal play area, with our centre of operations – the tree-house fortress. The tree-house was no more. In its place stood the Heights.

It was an ungainly building, with an emphatic roof, steep-pitched, French and fairy-tale-ish. The brickwork was pale ginger-bread, with two horizontal bands of red, like a sponge cake, double-layered and jam-filled. When the snow began to fall the roof acquired a dusting of icing sugar. A chimney stack piled up at the side of the house served as a buttress and fitfully puffed out smoke. Above the front door was a kind of balcony or oriel window, and on either side trellis work covered with spirals of dead clematis.

I pushed the letters mechanically towards the letter-box. It was boarded up. The letter-box was boarded over! I wasn't sure what to do. I shrugged and walked round the back. Four stone mushroom seats semi-circled a half-dug pit. Alongside was the upturned base of a blue-bottomed pond.

This was the clearing where Arfa had given practical expression to the skills we'd learnt at Scouts. We made a fire of twigs and fried three robin fledgelings on the lid of an old biscuit tin.

Julian, who had been Arfa's best friend and always followed a tongue's length behind him, betrayed us and told Mr Gunn, the scout master, who duly went spare. He shouted, swore and threatened to kill Arfa. He tore off Arfa's scout beret and trampled it under foot, saying it had been dishonoured. He tore off the knotted scarf and shirt badge. It didn't stop there – as perhaps it would have done with other people. Mr Gunn continued to rip off Arfa's clothes, his tirade of abuse giving way to gasps of endearment –'You wicked angel. What AM I going to do with you? I've never come across such exciting naughtiness in one so young.' It culminated in an attempted assault. In return for our silence the charges about the fledgelings were quietly dropped. Arfa became our leader. Our first act was to drag Julian to the boundary of our domain and try him under the Sacred Piss Tree.

I went back to the front of the house, and looked up to the oriel window. A woman's head popped out like a cuckoo-clock on cue and shouted, 'Wait there.'

I froze, called to heel. I supposed I'd spent too much time at the back of the house and was about to be told off. The voice had the grate of authority. I'd heard that tone so often as a child. Be grown up, it had said, be responsible mature, obedient, take our advice, learn from our experience and don't get taught the hard way. I thought as I got older I'd freed myself from having to hear it. I hadn't reckoned on a second helping as the rich lectured the poor, and the propertied glowered at trespassers. I could take it from my parents, even from older people. I had no choice at job interview panels, but not from the rich, especially the young ones, who seemed old in outlook and to have had no childhood.

Seconds later the woman appeared at the door. She said coldly 'The letter box is at the end of the drive.' Her eyes seemed to add, 'and not round the back.' Her tone went even further. 'You don't have to come right up to the house.'

She held her hand out for the letters, and gave a low grunt and nod as much as to say, 'I'll let it pass this time.'

'Thank you for telling me,' I said quietly, and when I was at a safe distance added aloud, 'Fuck you, too.'

I was glad I wouldn't have to go up to the house again. I didn't want to be made to feel a trespasser in an area we'd once ruled. The post-box, just as she'd said, was at the end of the drive, nailed four foot up the trunk of the Sacred Piss Tree. I'd mistaken it for a bird-box. It was shaped like a little house, with a vertical flap for the front door, that looked as if it might castrate my fingers.

'Come and get us!' came a shout in front.

Oh, not again!

'You'll never find us!'

So you think I don't know my way around here? Huh! Even with all the changes I know it better than you do! You wouldn't have got away from us.

'Come and find us!'

We used to dig pits here at the boundary of our domain and cover them with twigs and leaves so the rival gangs would fall in.

'Come on!'

I didn't realise at the time that this was just the sort of area – secluded and outskirty – where most murders happen. Or at least where most bodies are dumped. Lots of hollows and dells, shallow excavations not pursued by workmen, with fallen leaves gathered into corners, and the mouldy, mildew smell of quick rotting vegetation. I breathed in deeply; it was exhilarating. Just the area for a missing child. Wouldn't it be lovely if . . .?

'Come and find us.'

Why should I? You're not playing the sort of games I used to play.

'Come on! Come and get us.'

Come and get you? So you really want to play games? Real games? Good 'uns? Yeah, in those bushes where you're all going now. Wanna join in? Nice bit of pretend violence? That goes wrong? Wrong for you, that is.

'Goodbye,' called Robin.

Get lost. We used to fry robins.

'And don't come back,' added the eldest girl. 'Or Mummy will tell you off again.'

Shrivel up, tiny tits. I wouldn't even use your skull as a paper weight. I shook my fist at them. Bobby and Arfa and Julian and me don't want you here.

They dissolved into giggles and rustled the bushes. God. Small wonder the other postmen didn't want this round.

Next morning the Mummy Person was standing under the Sacred Piss Tree, rubbing her hands and stamping her feet, twittering at the edges like a hedge sparrow. Oh, God, I thought, she's going to tell me off.

Running round her were three King Charles Spaniels. She called them by names I couldn't quite make out, probably some affected literary illusion she'd culled from the Dictionary of Fictional Dogs, or some such mail order Book of the Month. But that's as may be, whatever she chose to call them I was quite happy to christen them – Widdles, Tiddles and Turds. They made a point of going right under the Sacred Post-box Tree. Nasty grudging little turds, neatly coiled and strangulated to a quiff.

Wouldn't it be lovely to put a stone in a snowball and lob it at them while they were still at stool? Imagine their pained expressions! Those back legs, stiff from crouching, awkwardly getting back into gear, their shit-caked tails held high!

Mummy looked at me as much as to say You're late. She added, aloud, 'You were quite right not to give the mail to the children yesterday. I didn't realise they had tried to get it off you.'

Yeah, I thought. I wouldn't trust them with anything. Nasty little brats, aren't they? What made you have 'em?

'It wasn't their fault. They thought you were going to put them in the box. They were only trying to help.'

Like fuck, I thought. If you believe that you can't have been a child yourself.

'Perhaps, after all, you could bring the post right up to the house,' she said and smiled.

'Alright,' I said aloud.

'I know it's further but, don't worry, I'll put some salt on the ice.' She seemed to thaw a little herself when saying this.

Don't bother, I thought. I've got my big boots on. It's your children who wanna be careful. 'Thank you,' I said aloud.

'I'm waiting for a particularly important . . .'

I handed her the mail, which she eagerly flicked through, her face registering disappointment. 'Are you sure that's all?' She glanced at the mailbag, which was empty. I still kept it strapped like a satchel across my chest.

'They don't mean any harm,' she said again. And she called the harmless cherubs to her. They ran up meekly, all innocence, and began to play happy families, and posed together as if I was going to take a snapshot of them.

I know what sort of shot I'd like to take. What was it Arfa used to say? 'Crumple, you scum, and let the snow do the burying.'

The weather was getting worse and I was feeling the effects of the cold. I took the next few days off but as I wasn't paid for sick leave I returned before I was really better. At the sorting office I found that none of the mail for the Enclave had been delivered in my absence.

The Heights looked deserted. All the curtains were drawn. There were no footprints in the snow. I assumed the children were confined to the house. I soon heard them shouting and clapping from the oriel window.

'He's coming. He's coming.'

I looked round expecting to see their father behind me.

'Here he is.'

'He's coming, Mummy. You go.'

'No, you go, darling.'

'But Mummy, he likes you best.'

'Have you got it this time?'

'Have you got it?'

'Mummy says we have to have it.'

Well, that a change! No more territorial reprimands now! I almost felt like the breadwinner, bringing in the hunting trophies from afar to their now contracting and apparently fatherless world. I heard the door bolts unlock as I approached.

And there they stood. Mummy and kids, all dolorous, frozen at the door, numbed like rabbits in front of a stoat. They looked at me as if I was an executioner.

And how I'd like to have been! Wouldn't it be lovely to lock them in and then set to? A whole family unit. Get 'em all and then there's no-one left to tell.

The children sheltered behind the Fragile Mummy Figurine. Robin had put his head under her apron creating the effect of a low-slung pregnancy. Poor woman! She had a kind of damage limitation, be-gentle-with-me look in her eyes.

'Where have you been? We were so worried.'

That was nice of them, I supposed. I said I'd been ill. I expected them to ask me how I was.

'It meant we had to go without our letters.'

'Well, never mind,' I said. 'You've got a double lot now.' I handed her the mail. She flicked through it quickly.

'Tuh! You still haven't brought us the letter we've been waiting for.'

'No, I don't suppose I have,' I said, unconcernedly, and added under my breath, 'but then I'm not Father Christmas. I'm only an auxiliary postman.'

I opened the mailbag so they could all look in, and the same time I glanced over them into the hallway.

'We're very grateful to you. We'll invite you in when we're sorted.'

The evil little familiars smiled agreement. I was being lured into some trap. I felt their eyes on the back of my neck as I walked away.

The next delivery was after Christmas. I reckoned they'd have retreated indoors still further. It wouldn't be long before a disembodied hand beckoned through a chained-up door. But something was wrong. There were tyre marks along the path. The postbox had been removed from the tree. The house was deserted. The windows had been boarded up in a very official and professional way rather like the boarding the Council puts up in our block to prevent squatters.

I knocked loudly. The letter-box was not boarded. I looked through. The furniture was covered with off-white sheets – crumpled artistically to give a cob-web pattern.

They can't have gone. They would have told me. Perhaps it was a feint by the Murderer who'd slain them all. I looked in the pit by the mushroom seats. I looked under the upturned base of the pond. Then I remembered the pile of logs, where the tree house had been. I felt the cut at the ends. It was smooth. There had been no starting and stopping; they hadn't paused as they cut down our tree-house; it was all done in one go. There must be a chain-saw somewhere.

How I'd love to find it! And go berserk with it. And cut them down, too. In one go. See how you like it!

I searched for evidence. A bow from off a plait of platinum hair. A bobble from a woolly hat. Even a mitten, plaintively fingerless. There was nothing, not even one of the distinctive little dog turds.

Poor doggies! Perhaps they'd had their throats cut. Bloody good job, too! Yea, the first thing you gotta do is kill the dogs. Arfa hated dogs. He wasn't scared of them. He just hated 'em.

I toyed with going to the Police. A murder, a child molestation, a family terrorised to flight?

Was I a suspect? Yes? No?

WHY NOT?

I asked at another house, the Dell, only to be met with a stoney face from the woman who answered. 'I'd continue to deliver if I were you. I'm sure everything of importance will get forwarded.'

'Have they left then?'

'They told us nothing.'

'They didn't tell me, either.'

She looked at me as if to say −Why should they? You're only a postman?

I asked at the Dene. There was no one in. I went to the Hollow.

'Hadn't you heard?' gushed the lady, knowingly. 'It's the talk of the Enclave. I expect they were too ashamed to tell you.'

'Oh.'

'They must have thought you were their new regular postman and naturally didn't want you to know,' she explained. 'They didn't realise you were just one of the Christmas Temps. and would be going on to better things.'

'Oh, I see,' I said. She could hardly have made a more cutting remark.

'We only found out by chance. Tragic, isn't it? And at Christmas, too! Who'd have thought it possible? They've been repossessed!'

I didn't register at first. Did she mean they'd lapsed after being saved from a diabolic takeover.

'Pardon?'

'They've taken possession. The building society. They couldn't keep up the payments.'

'Oh? And is there a forwarding address?' I asked mechanically.

So that was the excuse the Mummy Person had given out. It could all be made to fit in − if you wanted to believe it. The glossy brochures not for investment but for loans. The foreign mail going progressively further afield for help. The tragic Mummy Figure desperate for the cheque to arrive before the notice to quit.

'Isn't it the saddest thing you've ever heard,' enthused the woman, the cold air bringing roses to her cheeks. 'And at Christmas, too! WHAT a New Year they'll have! We all thought he was doing so well at his job. And she was so at home. Even had her car registration number the same as the postcode. No-one suspected anything until . . . No, there's no forwarding address. Thank God, I say, the whole family's gone together.'

I'll second that, I thought, adding aloud, 'Yes it's best when it happens to them all.'

Yea, get' em altogether. Wouldn't it have been lovely to be one of the bailiffs? Much more fun being a removal man than a delivery man. Then I'd really have a good uniform. No-one would question my identity then. Go up and bang on the door. Wake 'em up. Before dawn. They'd soon have known what I wanted. Smashin' Yeah! Smashin' everythin' With big dogs, too. I mean real dogs. Big shitters.

Still I felt a bit hurt they hadn't said goodbye. They must have known what was on the cards. I'd been cheated of my chance to say Good Riddance.

We didn't mean it. Bobby and Arfa and Julian and me say you can come back.

I continued to deliver. I'd heard nothing official to say otherwise. It hardly mattered. Just mail shots. No cards, nothing official.

I'd have used the tree post-box if it'd still been there. The path to the house was very slippery. They were the only family that put salt on the ice. I'll say that for them.

On the very last delivery I made before being laid off I noticed the house seemed the worse for wear. A couple of slates had come off. The top run of brick banding didn't seem parallel to the other bands. The chimney buttress was almost detached.

Come on you trees, you creepers, thorns and briars. Weather it to a ruin. Revert to the wild. Clematis to old man's beard. Creep over and stifle the laburnum and the flowering, fruitless cherry.

Make it like it was!

Well our Feeble Frame …

Well our Feeble Frame ...

Alison Keyes was sitting on a bench in the port of Aqaba. For the first time on this holiday she felt free. She'd been the first down to breakfast, and the first out the hotel. There was no-one approaching her either way along the coastal path. And nothing to impede her view over the Red Sea.

The furthermost tips of four countries angle into this dead end spur. Saudi Arabia is furthest away, some twenty kilometres due south. Across the water lies the Sinai peninsula, accessible by ferry. And to the north, on a steep slope, the Israeli port of Eilat. Aqaba itself, the only port of Jordan, extends up the foothills behind. A marvellous enclosure of space, thought Alison. A suntrap, with the surrounding mountains changing colour, pink, grey, purple, and the sea a deep blue, dramatically scored with bright red oil tankers, up from the south. And with me, she laughed, at the centre. And not just geographically – historically as well.

She was not particularly religious, and yet it meant something that these four countries had given birth to or cradled the three great monotheistic religions. She liked to think of herself as a cerebral traveller. Crucial sites in the History of Thought meant more to her than palaces and pleasure gardens. She'd visited Florence, as the fons et origo of the Renaissance; Mainz as the birthplace of Gutenburg and the printed word; Wittenburg as the starting pistol of the Reformation. She'd stood in Bastille Square,

131

trying to visualise the symbol of oppression that had led to the French Revolution and to so many Modern Ideas.

She would love to have visited Saudi Arabia as the birthplace of Islam, but no tours operated there. She'd considered going to what some – not she – called the Holy Land, but go there, and you might be refused entry to neighbouring countries. Jerusalem must remain her final destination. As for Egypt, she'd made several excursions already. The first had been an organised tour which emphasised the biblical connections at the expense of Pharaonic history. On subsequent visits she'd travelled independently. She had no fear of getting lost. The Nile was an ever-present comfort. Over four holidays she'd followed its course from the cataract at Aswan through the shallows to Cairo, along the Rosetta branch of the Delta to its confluence with the sea. She had developed a relationship with the oldest life-giving continuum.

The Red Sea, too, had its attractions, with the four disparate countries sloping down as if to sip at a communal water hole. Each country vainly set imaginary boundaries in the water. Yet the shoals of fish swam freely, and the coral grew round every coastline. The sun did not observe borders or discriminate. It shone on everything and glistened on the sea enough to make your eyes smart. And, thought Alison, to blind you to the dangers that water can present.

She had no fear of flying, but was ambivalent about the sea. She'd been on cruises often enough, and thought them pretentious, mere floating hotels. She favoured smaller craft, and on the Nile had preferred feluccas to steamers. It was the act of boarding that posed the problem, going from land to water, the transfer of element. Once safely across she had no greater fear that the boat would be engulfed by water than that the dry land would be levelled by an earthquake. It was the gangplank aspect that frightened her. She shivered at the thought of a large ocean liner moored at the quayside and the deep ravine between the ship and the quay slowly widening and narrowing, the vessel sometimes nudging the quay, almost playfully, but enough to cause certain death for any poor soul who had fallen between the two. She always tested the solidity of gangplanks and temporary bridges. She was never the first to cross. Try though she had, she could never overcome this fear. She often woke at dead of night, gasping for breath, imagining the water raising her up even as the ship and quay crushed her from either side.

Happily, smaller craft held few such fears. Yesterday, for example, she'd gone with her tour party in a glass-bottomed boat to view the coral. The boat was so cramped and the chatter so off-putting she'd hardly seen anything. Today, she intended a repeat performance alone. If yesterday's trip had been a half-hour organised taster, today's would be two hours of self-indulgence.

She walked to the little harbour where the glass-bottomed boats were moored. The boat boys were just arriving, and one of them wasted no time in offering his services. She looked uncertainly at the boat. It was much smaller than the one yesterday. The makeshift gangplank was like a roofer's ladder nailed every half metre with footholds, and angled from the quayside over the shallow water to the back railings of the boat. It was precarious, but she walked it with dignity. She settled down on the slatted seats, and spread herself out.

She felt able to take off her hat. She had a small patch of psoriasis in the hair above her left temple. It was not conspicuous, but outdoors she always wore a hat against the sun or wind, and indoors often held her head in her hand, which gave her an intellectual appearance. She also had psoriasis on her elbows and knees. These patches were more noticeable. She wore long sleeves and dresses below knee-length – and that gave her an old-fashioned look.

Today, alone apart from the boat boy, she felt able to roll up her sleeves, and trail her arm in the water. The shiny surface of the psoriasis would not show if her arm was wet. She leaned over further, and could have touched the larger coral formations visible in the water. The boat boy thought she was trying to break a piece off. He offered to stop and get her a branch. She refused, slightly shocked, and changed position. He smiled and pointed downwards. She leaned forward to the glass panel. She had an uninterrupted view of the rainbow world of fish and coral, an aerial glimpse of a hidden world, an amazing revelatory world for which there was no evidence from the shoreline, less than ten metres away.

Occasionally the boat went aground. The boat boy revved the engine and reversed, and sent the fish scurrying. The propeller churned up the sand. It quickly settled. The boy insisted on wiping the glass panel. The fishes re-appeared, unconcerned. Alison leaned over still further. It was like opening your eyes under water to confirm the miracle. She wanted to dive into the panel and join the fish in a different element. The boat boy gauged her enthusiasm and offered to take her down the coast to a marina which ran scuba diving courses. She refused, tapping on her watch. She knew the courses would presume you could swim – which she could not.

She had taken swimming lessons, but without success. The town she lived in had two swimming pools. The one near her home was part of a sports complex, glass, aluminium, open plan save for the changing rooms. The pool was international size, always full of school classes and swimming clubs. Round three sides of the pool was a public viewing gallery, and on the fourth a glass-fronted restaurant. This was not the venue, she decided, for a woman of her years to learn to swim.

She went to the older, poorer part of town, to a Grade 2 listed building, the words Municipal Baths cut in the stonework high above the entrance steps. The pool was small and rarely used save by a few regulars. There was no café, just a broken vending machine. The woodwork, iron railings and the tiling were impressive and obviously made to last, though perhaps now in need of maintenance. The gallery was cordoned off with a sign 'Danger! No Admittance'.

Alison felt more at home here. She wouldn't be recognised this side of town. No-one she knew would see her psoriasis. She registered with a beginner's class. The lessons were held either in the children's pool, or in the shallow end of the main pool. She found she could hold onto the little gully in the tiles, stretch full length, paddle her feet and stay afloat, and she could do this facing up or down. She could immerse her head, cope with the taste of chlorine, with the water in her ears and up her nose. She could open her eyes underwater, and even hold her breath for some considerable time. But when it came to letting go, taking her legs off the bottom of the pool, she thrashed around, creating foam and spume.

The instructor gave her a float. 'Hold on with one arm and paddle with the other,' he called out from the edge of the pool, 'and do pick those feet up – and kick.' She pushed the float through the water, held on tightly, raised one leg and hopped. Even getting to the other side like this she took to be an achievement of sorts.

The instructor told her to look at the other beginners. Several, all younger, could manage a width without a float. She was not used to being a pupil, or being shown up in front of her juniors. She soon came to think her lack of progress was due to inadequate instruction – and the fact she was always being jostled in the water by the others.

'Go with the flow,' one of them advised. She was not sure what was meant. The pool was not running water or tidal.

She missed a couple of lessons and then forced herself to attend. The class was much smaller now. Some students had dropped out, and others progressed to improver level. The instructor sounded genuinely pleased to see her. He now joined the students in the water, which seemed to sober him, and put his own abilities to the test. He shouted less, and methodically revised the drills he'd taught the weeks she'd been away. He demonstrated 'treading water'. Alison was able to stretch out her arms, then embrace herself, then thrust out her chest and circle her arms again. But lifting her feet was too much. She raised one foot, readjusted her balance and arm strokes, and raised herself on her toes. Instead of treading down with her feet she began to paddle. She toppled backwards thrashed, splurted and spat. She refused to try again and spent the rest of the lesson holding onto the little gully in the tiles, face down and kicking out.

The instructor walked back with her to the changing rooms. He spoke encouragingly and was still waiting outside, shivering in his swimming trunks, when she emerged in her overcoat. He continued the conversation as if nothing had happened. She got the impression he was worried about the numbers in the class, even about the future of the building. 'See you next week,' he said, cheerily. 'You won't,' she thought.

She toyed with going back to the nearby modern pool, taking private lessons when few people were around. She'd pay the instructor to be patient. She never did and the longer she left it the more she found excuses for not going. She even came to believe she'd caught her psoriasis from the pool.

The boat boy was staring at her. He smiled and pointed to the glass bottom. There was a tank or jeep or some military vehicle that must have found its way from a local conflict. The fish seemed to like it and swam in and out of the contorted, rusting shell.

The boy waved to a large vessel some distance away and warned her to hold onto the rails. She couldn't understand why, till the wash hit them. The boat bobbed up and down in the swell. She let herself go with the turbulence and rested her arms on the rails. Then panicked how flimsy the boat was. A little water was seeping through the ill-fitting glass panel. She could see no life-raft, no life-jacket, no instructions what to do in an emergency. No bell. No registered name.

She looked at her watch. There was still plenty of time before she had to go back to her hotel and resume the tour. But her mood had changed, and she told the boy to head straight for the jetty. She rolled down her sleeves, and with some satisfaction put on her hat. She liked Muslim countries where you were expected to cover yourself. Even without the psoriasis she wouldn't have gone round scantily clothed. That sort of attitude and outlook, that sort of beach-based holiday, never appealed to her.

She had chosen this particular guided tour in the hope of getting to some out-of-the-way places, and then being left to look round them by herself. She'd made polite conversation to other tourists on the plane, or while queuing at Customs. In the hotel she kept her distance, took an early breakfast and sat at a single table. On the coach there was always enough room to get a window seat alone. She took her evening meal out of the hotel. At the end of the day she was truly grateful for having booked a single room, despite having to pay a supplement. A shiver of revulsion ran through her at the thought of sharing.

Getting on with people had never been a strong point. She'd been through several relationships and liaisons. She didn't choose to think or talk about them in detail anymore. She had no current ties and commitments. She had made a rule never to listen to other people's troubles, confide her own problems, pass on gossip or run anyone down. She stayed aloof, looked on, saw what she saw – and did not register.

Which was not to say she didn't sometimes get annoyed or even angry. For instance, she knew sooner or later she'd have to say something to the tour guide. He was too much. He was ever present, and never knew when to stop talking, or to confine himself to essential information. He was local, well-informed, took a pride in his job, and his English was admirable. He obviously meant well, was trying to be what he thought was helpful. But he never let up. From the very first, Alison knew she'd cross swords with him.

'My name is Taleb,' he'd said as he collected their passports at the hotel reception. 'There's another tour here. From another holiday company. It's important we stay together. They have been here two days already. So. They are the Settlers. And you. You are the Nomads. What are you?'

'The Nomads,' the group chorused in unison, with the exception of Alison.

'And who am I?' None of the group remembered his name, except Alison who said nothing.

The next morning on the walking tour of Aqaba, the group was counted out and called to heel with the aid of a multi-coloured golf umbrella. Alison hoped subsequent trips would be more relaxed. If they weren't she knew she would have to absent herself or say something. When the inevitable exchange occurred Alison was surprised at her own vehemence. It happened like this.

She was looking forward to the stay in Petra. It pleased her to be visiting an ancient civilisation that was neither Greek nor Roman, and one that for a time had resisted the advances of both. She was particularly fond of those ancient cultures that had opposed Rome. She'd spent holidays in Carthage and Etruria. She was intrigued that the original inhabitants of Petra, the ancient Nabateans, were descendants of the Edomites, one of the Twelve Tribes of the Bible, and that they'd left a physical, if not a spiritual, legacy comparable to the descendants of the most famous of those twelve tribes.

The tour coach arrived in Petra at night. The next morning was clear and crisp. Taleb suggested they wear warm clothing, and take water and a snack for the long walk ahead.

'We'll time the walk so we arrive at the end of the Souk when the sun's full on the façade of the Treasury.'

The Souk was a deep, narrow, winding ravine, where the sun rarely got a look-in save in the wider sections. There were a few spindly trees, and several side gulleys that were blocked off to prevent flash floods. Taleb stopped to describe all the carvings, monuments and features. At first everyone tuned in, but he proved almost too thorough. Several of the party drifted off, some went ahead of him and relied on their guide books. Others held back taking photos, and even those who remained stamped their feet and hugged themselves to keep warm. Alison, thankful she'd worn a thick cardigan, stayed at the end of the group, just within earshot. Taleb didn't seem too worried by this lapse of attention. He was more concerned about another tour party which was getting too close. On one occasion, both tour guides ended up describing the same monument at the same time. There was a decided friction and a raising of voices. Alison listened in to the rival guide and found his more relaxed delivery far preferable. However, she was not allowed to linger, and was jiffied along.

'Come on, Nomads. A few more minutes and we'll be in the sun.'

Alison could understand why Taleb wanted to get the timing right, so that the impact of seeing the Treasury in the right light would be maximised. She knew the Souk ended in a T-junction with a wider, sunnier ravine, on whose surface had been carved a magnificent façade. She'd learnt from her guide books that the exit to the Souk was not quite at ninety degrees to the ravine, nor the façade immediately opposite the exit, nor were the sides of the Souk straight enough to form a symmetrical frame for the façade – and yet from innumerable glossy photographs, contrasting the darkened Souk and the brilliantly lit detail of the façade, she knew that one's first sighting would be a rare revelatory moment to be treasured for life. Seeing it in actuality, three-dimensional, its scale, the rosy-tint of the stone, coming out into the open and the warmth of the sun after the chilly confined Souk, would be a total experience that no film or photo could ever match. She anticipated this moment and knew that it would not disappoint.

The gorge wound along and the sides became less vertical and more contorted. The tour party in front had slowed down; the party behind had caught up. Taleb held up his umbrella. 'We are nearly there.' He checked his watch and beckoned them on slowly. The gorge narrowed and darkened still further. Then like a jagged bolt of lightning the phosphorescent pink façade, finely carved and classic in intent, contrasted with the rude, cold, winding disorder of the Souk. It was an unexpected vision that had no right to be there – and yet undeniably, magnificently, was.

Alison stood enrapt, oblivious to all around her, her spirits lifted, warmed inwardly by the sight, and outwardly by the sun. Then she felt something pluck at the sleeve of her cardigan, on the elbow, right on the patch of psoriasis. It was the Taleb.

'Come over here, will you, please. With the other Nomads. Then I can tell you about it. You can take photos later.'

Something in her snapped. She came down to earth. She out-stared the guide and in a quiet voice, and with the minimum of gesture, she enunciated clearly. 'You have seen this a thousand times. This is my first. I've travelled half-way across the world. This is just down the road for you. For me, this is an ambition fulfilled, a dream come true. I do not need you to tell me what to look at. Or when I can and cannot take a photograph. Let there be nothing between me and it. Least of all – you.'

There were several tourists within earshot, but none from her group, and none talking English, or who appeared to have understood what she'd said. She looked back at the façade. The spell had gone, never to be recaptured.

She spent the rest of the time in Petra finding her own way around. She preferred to do this anyway, but realised she'd set herself apart. She couldn't worry. Sooner or later the other members of the group would also tire of the guide.

She'd have liked to have stayed at Petra and let the tour go on without her. She couldn't help feeling that it was the high spot of the holiday and the rest of the itinerary would be mere padding. True, the Roman ruins at Jerash proved impressive in size, as always with Rome, but they didn't add much to other Roman ruins she'd seen throughout the Mediterranean. The coach stopped briefly at two different sites, both claiming to be the Spring of Moses. Alison didn't feel any particular frisson that she might be walking – millennia later – in his sadly eroded footsteps. These days her conception of Moses was conjured up less from the sacred texts than from his appearance in sculpture, paintings and opera.

Her reaction was different when they stopped at Mount Nebo. She had heard of it for the first time from the tour itinerary. She felt she should have heard of it before. Perhaps she had and couldn't recall it. Seemingly Moses had looked from Mount Nebo across the Dead Sea to the Promised Land. Taleb said that on a clear day you could see the towers of Jerusalem. Alison couldn't see anything, and wasn't going to use her binoculars to look into the setting sun.

High on the promontory was an information point, a long raised metal panel rather like a lectern, on which were etched the names of towns, arrows pointing in their direction, with the distance in kilometres. Hebron, Bethlehem, Ramallah, Jericho, Nablus, Jerusalem, Herodium, Lake Tiberias. She stood there, leaning on the lectern, her arms wide apart, her head nodding as she read the names and followed the signs. Each place-name resonated – from her schooldays, scripture classes or morning assembly, some from the history of the Roman occupation, some from current news bulletins. There was no-one around and she felt moved to read the names aloud, in her clear, bell-like enunciation. 'Hebron. Bethlehem. Ramallah. Jericho.' After each she looked over in the direction of the town, which she couldn't see clearly because of the haze. She felt as if she were addressing an imaginary audience. 'Nablus. Jerusalem. Herodium. Lake Tiberias.' It was like repeating after a teacher, new words in a foreign language, committing them to memory, not knowing their full meaning but being impressed with the sound and her ability to repeat it.

She was the last tourist to leave the site. Taleb was coming to fetch her.

'I'm sorry,' she said. It was the first time they'd spoken for days.

Someone on the coach said, 'Carried away, were we, taking photees?' She smiled, said nothing, and settled down for the long drive to Amman.

She had high hopes of the capital. She'd lose the coach party and walk round the sights and markets by herself. She'd eat at local restaurants. She hoped the privations of small-town accommodation were over, and the hotel would be modern and luxurious. Seemingly the holiday company had obtained a special off-season deal, which in effect meant double rooms en suite at single room prices. She checked the bathroom. What a contrast with the pit-stops at Aqaba and Petra. Newly tiled, no damp stains on the walls, no rusted taps, corroded with limescale. Thick-fleeced towels, hand to bath size, and a little basket of miniatures – soap, shampoo, shower gel, bath foam – each individualised with the hotel logo. The water pressure wasn't the usual grudging dribble, but a full flow, that got hot quickly. The shower rose wasn't bunged up, and the jet was strong enough for a water massage. The bath – in the other hotels there had only been a shower – was deep, with in-built rungs and a bar support on the wall. Alison loved taking a bath, a full hot bath, and after the privations of coach travel one would be particularly welcome. She'd never believed that virtue is achieved by needless denial. She never really subscribed to the Cleanliness and Godliness ethic, nor to Cold Shower and Resolve. But a good freshen up and soak never went amiss.

There was no time for a bath now. She planned to skip the evening meal and begin her jaunt of the city. She went down to the hotel foyer and bumped into some of the tour group trailing into the restaurant.

'Aren't you coming to dinner?'

'Not tonight, no.'

'Going out?'

'Yes.' She watched them troop into the dining hall.

Many of the shops in the foyer were still open. Most sold tourist items and souvenirs. One was devoted to beauty treatments. Normally Alison wouldn't have taken much note, but the product ranges here were not international names, with designer bottles, and elaborate packaging embossed with crests, but locally produced items – mud soap, shampoo, local scent, bath crystals – all made from natural ingredients, mainly from the Dead Sea. They claimed unique properties for rejuvenation and for dealing with a variety of skin complaints, including psoriasis. She bought a selection – in the smallest quantities available, some little more than phials and testers. She took them back to her room and was tempted to try a couple before going out.

She washed her hands with the mud soap. It darkened them and left a tidemark in the washbasin. She blackened her eyebrows, and laughed at the transformation. She wetted her hair. She'd never had dark hair and had never thought to dye it, not even when it began to grey. The mud soap darkened it completely. She couldn't believe how different she looked. She went back and forth from the bedroom mirror to the one in the bathroom. She held the towel round her neck to accentuate the contrast. She wanted to be photographed like this.

Soon the soap began to dry and cake, and to feel heavy and taut. She was about to wash it off in the sink. Or should she have a shower? Or a bath? She knew if she had a bath that her expedition to town wouldn't happen. Nonetheless, she opted for a bath. There could be few people having a bath this time of night so the water pressure would be strong, and the water hot. She ran a full bath and added the miniature of bath foam. She looked at the phial of Dead Sea Crystals she'd bought. It said use the lot, which seemed rather excessive, but she did.

She lowered herself gingerly into the bath. The supports were invaluable. She settled, lay back, until she was submersed save for her head, the foam forming a fur collar, an effervescing ruff. She gave a sigh of seismic proportions. Quite unbidden the words of a hymn came to her "Well our feeble frame He knows."

She adjusted herself and let her arms float freely. The bath was deep enough for her to sit up, stretch her arms on the bath edges and let her legs float. She wished she could float totally. She lathered herself with the mud soap and the bubbles of the bath foam disappeared, and the soap left a tide-mark on her. She would definitely have to shower afterwards. She was in no hurry to get out.

Next morning she awoke and felt more at ease than at any time in the holiday. The psoriasis on her elbows had abated, the redness had reduced, even the bumpiness was less apparent. She double-checked her knees and temple. They, too, were much improved. She wanted to put it down to the crystals, but dismissed the idea. It was relaxation. That was all. Psoriasis reacted unfavourably to heat, tight clothing and stress. It might only be a temporary remission, that might cease once the touring resumed.

Yet need it be? She must test the crystals full strength. She'd used them all up. She didn't know when the hotel shops opened. Her party was assembling in the foyer for the guided tour of Amman. She smiled at them.

'Not coming?' one of them said.

'No,' she replied.

'Oh. Saw it all yesterday evening, did we?'

'Something like that.'

She had the shops to herself and lingered over the products, reading all the labels. She bought more than she reckoned, in particular the crystals. They were plain, transparent, not artificially coloured or scented, with no additives. Any blending was caused by geological fusions, millions of years ago. The only processing was in the extraction.

She went back to her room and dissolved some crystals in a little water. She dabbed her elbows and knees. And to help them dry she waved her arms and stood on one leg and waved the other. Her movements regularised and resembled practice for swimming. She convinced herself the skin in the affected areas was even smoother.

Also her joints did not ache. Was that because she had rested? Bathed? Used the crystals? Or because psoriasis was the outward expression and precursor of some incipient deep-seated malaise, such as gout or rheumatism – and the cure for the surface affliction helped eradicate the deeper one? Did crystals placed on the surface of the skin somehow draw out the gout crystals from the joints? She had no medical evidence for this. That didn't matter to her. She didn't think that just because her mother had had psoriasis in the self-same places that the complaint was hereditary. She believed it could be infectious. Many people thought so. It looked infectious and one reason for hiding it was to avoid being shunned. She was convinced she had caught the psoriasis in the swimming pool, just in the way you could pick up verrucas and other infections. But if, she reasoned, she'd caught psoriasis from immersing herself in water, then surely – as with the prevention of disease and the whole rationale behind inoculation – was not the cure the very same element as the catching? Albeit in smaller, more concentrated quantities? The cure for something caught from water would be further immersion – in water, enriched by curative substances.

Images flashed through her mind. A holiday devoted to taking the water cure. A tour of the Bads in Germany, the Terme in Italy, even the Spas in England? But how much better the place from where these crystals came? The Dead Sea itself, the most natural bath of all, with none of the incongruity of hot springs in a cold climate. Out in the open, not an enclosure built over a subterranean flooded cavern or a fanciful grotto, not waters piped and canalised to a suitable surface location and then made into an artificial basin, with adjacent casinos. No, a natural phenomenon, an oasis unfit to drink, but which would buoy you up even if you were unable to swim, where the minerals would be full-strength, far more so than in commercial products. The prevention and cure came from an inland sea, that was called dead but which had life-enhancing properties, and was by chance part-located in what was known as the Holy Land. It was not religion or local history that effected the cure – but immersion and baptism – which happened to be a ritual in one of the three great religions born in this area.

Alison herself had never been baptised. She was registered at birth as Christian, Church of England. Her parents rarely attended church. She could recall them going to weddings and funerals, but not, to her knowledge, to christenings. She'd been born at the end of the War when it wasn't a light undertaking to take a baby to the local church and immerse it naked in cold water. She wasn't told she'd not been baptised until she was nearly ten, too young to understand what it all meant and far too young to organise it herself. She toyed with the subject again in her early teens when a mild religious inclination had overcome her. It did not last, and she had never pursued the matter.

The next stage of the tour itinerary – which involved a brief visit to the Dead Sea – now assumed greater importance for her. The schedule read "Leave mid-morning and drive to the Dead Sea. Stop for bathing and meal. Then long drive back to Aqaba. Followed by one free day, with an optional tour to Wadi Rhum. Flight home."

The stop at the Dead Sea was a mere four hours. She'd once thought it a piece of tokenism, an optional extra, a joke almost. Now it had become the main objective, the raison d'être, of the whole holiday.

'The lowest point on Earth,' Taleb began, as the coach hit the high road out of Amman. 'The water level is going down. Why is it going down? The River Jordan flows into it. There is no outlet. So why doesn't it overflow? Why is the water level going down?' He paused momentarily for anyone on the coach to answer. 'It is going down because evaporation is great. Hence the haze. Another decade and it may well be gone altogether.'

Surely not! Alison could hardly believe that. Something as permanent as the Dead Sea, a wonder of the world? A unique geological and historical feature? Common knowledge now, that might in the future require an explanatory footnote?

'Yes,' continued Taleb. 'The natural boundary between Jordan and Israel would go. There'd be a rush to claim mineral rights and territory. Nothing would grow, any more than in the desert. But once they'd excavated all the mineral wealth they'd build there – as they have in the desert. Imagine it – Dead Sea Estate, Dead Sea Settlement, 221b Dead Sea Mews.'

He paused for laughter. None came.

'Anyway, that's as may be. On a clear day you can see Jerusalem. The minarets and spires. Even the sun on the golden Dome of the Rock – well, at least, the sun catching particles of pollution – or the blades of a helicopter gunship.'

Alison looked across the Sea. She could see the other side. It wasn't far, just a change in the colour of the haze. She couldn't see Jerusalem, and she didn't mind. She was happy to be, in a country that took its name from its main river. Few other countries in the world did that. It meant something – surely?

146

'A warning,' said Taleb. 'If you intend to bathe you can hire a hut, towels, and swim wear. Very cheap, clean, all sizes. Umbrellas, too. You cannot swim naked. That's not allowed. Be careful not to stay in too long. You will float automatically. Don't roll over or try to swim. Don't get water in your eyes, or in cuts or scratches. Have a shower immediately afterwards. Be back at the coach in four hours.'

Alison hired a swim suit, changed in a cubicle and then put her blouse and skirt back on. She set off with the towel in her bag. The beach was about a kilometre long, quite artificial. The sloping sand had been transported from the desert. Large palms had been decanted, and around them were sunshades and deck chairs. There were open showers, worked by pulling at a kind of lavatory chain. They were popular with the local youths. Many tourists were photographing relatives in the water.

Alison went to the far end of the beach. She looked over the barbed-wire boundary fence to the original shoreline – irregular stones, encrusted with salt deposits, little rock pools iced round with salt. She stared across the hazy, boatless expanse of water. There were no sea-birds or noises from the far side. Even the sounds from this side were muted by the haze. And yet it was still a marvel that this water, which did not support life, could by its properties renew hers. Properties, that is, in the sense of contents and potential, as conjured up in the quasi-biblical descriptions in herbals. "It hath propertyes to deal with the quinsye and all manner of ague." Yes, she thought, the chemical suspensions buoy you up even as they cure you.

She took off her hat, kicked off her sandals, slipped off her blouse and skirt and put them neatly in her bag, which she left as near as she could to the water's edge.

She dunked in a big toe. The water was warmer than any of the swimming pools she had known, and smelt of salt rather than industrial chlorine.

She had been assured that here everyone can float. Let me not be the exception. Let this baptism be the cure for my complaints, scotch future ailments, and overcome previous humiliations.

She waded in. It was an effort, the water was heavy. When it was up to her thighs she bent her knees a little, leaned forward and stretched out an arm. It felt buoyed up. She looked back to the beach. She could see no-one near. She felt sufficiently relaxed and confident to squat down, lean back, take her legs off the seabed and stretch them out.

Then something happened. She was face-down and unable to turn round, the reverse of a beetle on its back, like a whale, floundering and threshing in its death agonies, waiting for the grappling hooks to hoist it on board.

She thought she was going under. She actually wished she could. She longed to disappear from view, but kept bobbing up and down. When her head sunk from air to water, the rest of her body sank from water to air, and vice versa. It was like waking up to find the dream still continuing, falling asleep again and only partly recapturing the first dream as a second, even worse, one came along. Her mouth filled with putrid-tasting water. She could only splutter not shout. It was some time before her odd gyrations were noticed. She was taken, half-conscious, to the nearest hut, in a state of extreme cramp or seizure. Her arms and legs were sticking out like a cow on a foot-and-mouth pyre. She was swaddled in towelling, and laid flat on a brightly-coloured lilo.

'Wash her down,' the doctor told the nurses. 'Keep her warm.'

Her skin was shiny with mineral slime. It was dabbed, then sluiced with a small spray of warm soapy water. The slime had accumulated worst in the angles of the joints. Crystals had formed across the eyelashes, binding the lids together, far tighter than early morning sleep, and certainly not to be dislodged with a rub from the back of the hand or a gentle scoop from a finger nail. A small-nozzled air spray dislodged any loose material, and a tepid water spray dissolved any remaining crystals.

When her eyes opened the doctor said, 'You were very lucky.'

Alison looked around.

'Yes,' the doctor continued. 'Very lucky, indeed. Took some doing on your part. Haven't had a case like this for years. And then it's usually a child.'

'Really,' said Alison coldly.

'It wasn't so much the water,' said the doctor, 'though that didn't help. Everything in you – temporarily – went. As if you'd completely let yourself go – and not even resisted when life began to ebb away. Your breathing stopped, your temperature plummeted and you seized up tighter than in rigor mortis. We thought you were a goner. Then you began shivering uncontrollably. You actually shivered your way back to life.'

'Did I?' she said.

'It was a small miracle. In its way.'

'Was it?'

'Let me know if ...'

'I shall be perfectly alright, thank you. Perhaps you could leave me to put on my clothes in privacy.'

The coach was delayed. 'What's the problem?' someone asked. Someone else pointed to the empty seat. 'Oh, her. Again.'

Alison was led back to the coach, swaddled in a rug, a blanket over her head, like a criminal, the doctor on one side, Taleb on the other.

'There you go,' the doctor said, as she was unceremoniously plonked down in her usual seat. He waved her goodbye. And without further delay the coach set off and Taleb began his commentary.

'On the right – the last chance to glimpse Jerusalem ... and the Dead Sea ... on the left the Moab mountains.'

Back in the hotel in Aqaba Alison slept through to mid-morning. She looked in the mirror. She was shiny red as if the psoriasis had spread all over her body. She didn't go down to breakfast. She was in two minds whether to go that afternoon on the optional excursion to Wadi Rhum. She felt she ought to make an appearance. She wore jeans, a long-sleeved blouse, and took a coat against the evening cold in the desert.

She made her way down to the hotel foyer. Taleb was already there. He seemed surprised to see her. Alison fully expected him to make some mock solicitous remark. He just said, 'Good to see you.' He had few takers for this trip and was grateful for the extra statistic. He called out to the other tourists. 'We have sufficient numbers now. The trip can go ahead.' The tourists gave Alison a little round of applause and clambered into the coach.

She followed them cautiously. During the holiday she had observed them group and regroup, change their positions at the breakfast tables and their partners on the coach. She moved down the aisle to her usual position.

'Glad you're OK,' said the couple in front. Alison wanted to say, 'Why should you suppose I have ever been anything but?' She restrained herself and said, 'I am, yes.' She couldn't resist adding frostily, 'And yourselves?'

And to her surprise they replied. 'I can't stand this heat, you know. Years ago I developed …' Alison did not quite catch the name of the complaint.

'And I have to be very careful. I'm on a course of …' She did not take in the name of the drug.

'And the pace of it all, doesn't help, does it?' another chimed in.

'Pretty relentless,' said another, and added, pointing to the guide, 'To say nothing of our friend. I call him Motor-Mouth. Gives me bloody ear-ache.'

They were off on a litany of woes that went well beyond a few gripes about this or that hotel or official. She'd never seen them so talkative and heated. It was if she, who'd remained aloof, who'd been ahead of them in her criticisms, who'd been publicly humiliated, was to be the one who inadvertently cracked the dam. She wasn't sure how to react. 'Oh, dear,' was all she could muster. She was almost glad when the tinny microphone whistled and Taleb began –

'Can you hear me at the back?'

'No,' came the reply, 'but don't worry.'

Taleb continued, 'We're driving to the desert. Which is beautiful. You will go in jeeps, six persons in each. We will drive round. See places. And we will watch the sun set. It will be a good day.'

'Hope so,' someone murmured.

'And,' Taleb went on, 'when the sun is setting we will be quiet and listen to the silence. To the desert silence. It is like ...' He paused, lost for a word.

'Yes?'

'Nothing else.' He clapped his hands and said in a different tone, 'Nothing else.'

'That mean he's finished?' asked the voice from the back.

There were many coaches from other hotels heading to the Wadi. At the terminus jeeps were lined up in readiness. 'Keep together, Nomads,' shouted Taleb as they decanted from coach to jeep. There was only just enough room to sit. It was very cold and when the jeeps got up speed the wind howled and drowned the engine noise and made it impossible to hear anything said. The scenery was breathtaking, awe-inspiring and did not need elucidating.

Several jeeps had a race over the sands. Alison was grateful that the driver in her jeep, maintained a steady pace. Her jeep was soon overtaken by all the others. Alison was able to look back onto an un-peopled desert. She supposed there was radio contact.

They turned into a side valley and in the distance she saw the other jeeps. She couldn't quite make out what was going on. Dozens of people from the jeeps had climbed up the rock to different levels and were facing the setting sun. It was like a biblical epic, a film set for the Second Coming.

Taleb helped them out the jeep and said, 'Nomads, we'll be here till the sun sets. Then I want you to stay and for five minutes not say anything – just listen to the desert silence. Is that OK?'

Alison thought that was a noble gesture – to be silent and contemplate the millions of years the rocks had been here, as against the mere hundred generations of humans. She assumed Taleb had been brought up near a desert and was trying to convey something of what it had meant to him in childhood and adult life. It was considerate of him and she respected him for it.

She climbed a short way up the rock to a position from where no-one was obscuring her view. The sunset was impressive, but not as beautiful as in some photos. She took a snap – as a memory jogger, and to prove she had been there. Then within minutes the light reduced, and the distant rocky outcrops lost their three-dimensionality and become silhouettes, starkly and darkly contrasting with the red sky.

'That's it,' Taleb said. 'And now five minutes to hear the desert silence. Shh! Shh! Listen to the silence.'

Alison could see his point. He was right to try … and she would have been sorry to see him fail. But the tourists from other groups appeared unaware what was expected of them. Even the other guides seemed to think the request faintly ridiculous. Several were smoking or eating sandwiches. Taleb held up his arms, patted the air as if trying to hasten a slowly deflating balloon. He put his finger to his lips. It was probably a futile expectation. Alison felt for him, but she wasn't going to join in the shushing.

Even so, the silence was deep and strangely contagious. She tried to predict what each minute of silence was going to be like. The first minute would still echo with Taleb's request for silence. The second minute would be a conscious attempt to focus the mind and let it rise above all forms of control. The third to rise above one's breathing, the blood pumping behind the ears, to ignore the fly that settles on you, the slight breeze that blows your hair in your eyes – and surely that minute would seem longer as one forgot the mechanical counting of time, and the fourth minute, however short, in human measurable terms, would be an eternity when you tuned full-volume into the apparent Presence of Nothing. The clap of Taleb's hands – 'That's it!' – was the five minute awakening from hypnosis.

And the stark realisation how cold it was. How hungry and tired she was. She'd have liked to stay longer. But to be stranded here at night – or at any time – would be a death sentence.

She doubted she'd ever come back. She supposed the silence must exist in other places as well.

Consequences

Consequences

No-one knew anything about his past – except this.

During the war he was in a house when it was bombed. All his relatives were killed.

Thereafter he was unable to live indoors.

That's all.

I am not sure why this 'story' appealed to me. I kept thinking about it. I tried to piece bits together, from observation, reliable information, but mainly speculation.

Harry – as he is now known – lives in a wood, or rather an enclave of urban woodland on a slope in South London. It is overlooked by houses with spacious gardens, and dominated by a radio mast that transmits world news throughout Southern England. It is also a perfunctory nature trail, suitably signposted, an example of local gesture politics. Children and dogs play and exercise in the wood. By night it has a reputation as a quiet place for furtive activities.

The first sighting of Harry can be disconcerting. Physically he is tall, silent, thick-set, and moves quickly. There is no awkward zombie stomp. He does not come across as a simpleton. But parents call their young children away. Older children come to taunt him, but soon lose interest. Dogs, at first hostile, ignore him. He sometimes annoys 'courting' couples. He always stands at a safe distance, looking on with an intent face. He never tries to join in, and never unzips himself. The only time he was ever known to have resorted to violence was when a tramp moved in to share his territory.

Several clumps of bushes, overgrown with ivy and other trailers, have been hollowed out and made habitable. Each one is strewn with silver paper he's collected. He sometimes rests in an electricity way-station, a kind of above-ground shelter, without windows and now with its door off, his body inside, his head pillowed on the doorstep.

He is said to live off berries and know the different types of fungi. He helps himself to the windfalls that fall his side of the garden fences. He never goes into the greenhouses or sheds. He is given food by an old lady who comes everyday to feed the wild birds and squirrels. She leaves a bag of food for Harry under a log. He is occasionally given money, which he spends at the local corner shop. He stands outside until the assistant comes and asks him to point to the items he wants. It's a mutual arrangement. Harry doesn't want to go inside. The shop-keeper doesn't want him in.

There's no way of telling whether he's been disadvantaged from youth, unhinged as a result of the bombing, or just appears outcast after years of isolation. He never speaks. He may be dumb – from whatever reason. He has a penetrating eye that is bright and alert, and not a bit as censorious as those who stare at him.

There's no possibility of my getting to know him, just by looking for some clue and insight, like peeping over a modesty shield for a glimpse of what is usually kept hidden. The best I can do is to use what I know, invent what I don't and work his life, not into a biography, but a short story. It has proved difficult.

My first attempt was protective and defensive. I had 'discovered' him. I decided to write about him from the angle I thought would reveal most – that of the placid life in some way disrupted, and his reaction to the change. There were several possibilities. The most obvious was to outdo my potential rivals-in-concern.

Harry is visited by a psychiatrist, who wants to 'cure' him; by a sociologist who wants to 'integrate' him, and by a more than usually appalling television crew 'doing' the odd-spots and odd characters of London. None succeed.

Nor even the philanthropist who makes him the sole benefactor of his will. A trust is set up to administer the legacy. Harry is properly fed and clothed. Housing he refuses. He would rather be left alone. He is no more particular in his habits than previously. And nor are the trustees who use his money for other purposes, and lose contact. He is attacked by muggers, who've heard a rumour he's rich and has a secret hoard. He's unable to throw them off though he knows every path and every overhang of bushes. He unwittingly leads them to his innermost retreat, the place with all the silver paper. They demand money. He points to the silver paper. They are incensed and beat him up. He is found and taken to hospital. He soon 'discharges' himself, leaves behind his number tag and all his would-be helpers. He returns, by some unerring instinct, to his place below the radio mast. He dies of cold. Or gets killed by a falling tree. His body is not discovered for some while. The role of the trustees is questioned, but the case is never fully pursued.

Now this might make a passable, potted, blow-by-blow history, though death should not be thought a fitting or wished-for ending for those whom we perceive as different or brand 'inadequate'.

There are other possible disruption stories. For example, the land around the radio mast is sold off to developers who 'evict' him. He returns and wanders like a ghost round the new toy-town estate, annoying the but-lately-installed residents. He is eventually accused of theft, rape, child molestation, etc and for want of a better suspect, etc. etc. All with tragic consequences.

Perhaps better might be a change coming from inside Harry himself. He overcomes his fear of going indoors. He sleeps right inside the way-station. He goes into the sheds and greenhouses. He expects to be invited into homes. He goes into the shop. He demands to be housed by the Council. Attitudes to him change very rapidly. Opportunities for satire here.

So what if he were taken seriously? If the 'gap' in his character was filled by putting him in a broader context, integrating him into a longer story, comparing and contrasting him with 'normal' society, and making him but one of many characters, an oddity who nonetheless turns out to have a crucial role. There is something reassuring, isn't there, about the outsider coming into his own, being consulted when all other leads have failed, a simpleton being the repository of knowledge, almost the hermetic life leading to curative powers?

The best format for this approach is a crime novel, one where the investigator doubles as a writer and sociologist, mapping out the underside of society. Harry is thought to have been a witness to a murder committed on 'his' territory. He now gains status by having no fixed abode. Many questions need to be answered. Was the body dumped? Or murdered in situ? The victim, according to the media, had everything to live for, was young, innocent, full of promise, loved by everyone, a saint-in-embryo, as well as being a possible future prime minister before the age of thirty. Who could possibly have wanted to kill someone like that?

Rewards are offered. None are claimed. All leads fail. The police come back to the woodland time and time again. Harry is taken in as a possible witness, and kept as the chief suspect.

He is dumb and cannot tell anything. Does he know anything? Neither the investigator nor the police can find out for certain. Harry is not sure what's going on, what he's supposed to have done. He has no identity and is not permitted to appear in court, either as a witness or defendant, or even in an identity parade.

The police are under pressure to make a conviction. The relatives of the saintly victim have appeared on every news bulletin for weeks, weeping and wailing. The local residents are up in arms. They've always had their doubts about Harry. Everybody is coming towards him, mouthing, gesticulating, smiling, reassuring, tempting. Harry is put away, whether as criminal or insane, or for his own safety hardly mattering.

He is stripped and immured in a cell. All the fears of being indoors, and of being trapped, return to him. The door clangs, the key grates and echoes. In the sound of the key all the sounds of the bomb exploding return to him.

He is a child again, back in his house just before it is bombed. He – I'll spare here a use of the first person; I'll not put words into his mouth – he does not hear the sound of the bomb exploding, but of other familiar household items being dislodged and broken. They jump up slightly from their accepted locations before beginning their final journey as whole objects. Objects implode towards him, as if magnetism has replaced gravity. All the containers in falling unscrew their lids, upturn and empty their contents over him. The cutlery drawer aims itself at him, blades first. Only the springs of the sofa defy the pattern and leap up.

The sounds do not come simultaneously, but are not quite antiphonal. Each object has its own particular resonance. All the synonyms for the word sound are represented, as are differences in tone and pitch between the breaking of similar substances, between a pane of glass, a glass bowl, a mirror and the stem of a drinking glass.

There is, too, a sequence of sounds – a falling chimney crashing through the ceiling and down through the floor, or brickwork partly dislodging a shelf and the items on the shelf relocating themselves according to their size, shape and weight, slowly at first then at a stampede. There is also the anticipation of further sounds – supporting items that will soon give way, the groaning legs of tables and chairs or the tautening and raising of pitch of stretched wire. There is the prolongation of sound, a saucepan lid clattering down, rebounding, rolling and spinning before being flattened by something else. And, of course, there are things which make no sound though expected to – the back door, locked and bolted against intruders, giving way noiselessly.

Above all is the fear where things will fall. Many items seem deflected in their descent. They do not fall where they might reasonably be expected to. The furniture has a mind of its own and regroups of its own volition. A table from upstairs crashes through the ceiling and lands neatly next to the chairs downstairs. The wallpaper strips itself and re-papers the pile of bricks below.

Leaves from a dismembered book, aerated and indecisive, ponder where they should fall and add their weight of commentary. Then plaster dust, as if in approval, settles like snow – deep and crisp and even – deadening all sound.

Without moving, being able to move, he echo-locates where everything has ended up. It is a change round of furniture. Had his parents always kept him out of a room that was being redecorated? Was he told to stop getting under their feet? He had no say in the matter then, and the same now.

I, myself – and I am not here being tempted into the first person and putting words into Harry's mouth – I remember the day when we moved house. I was only four at the time. We were moving from one end of the country to the other. We arrived late. It was mid-winter and had been snowing. We fitted the furniture in haphazardly – familiar furniture in different rooms, differently laid out. We unpacked a few of the smaller items; several had been broken or damaged in transit.

It had been a long day, and a complete uprooting. I was bewildered and couldn't find my way round the house. I could not gauge distances. Items of furniture seemed to have changed size in their new settings. I stayed up far later than usual. For the first time in my life I had a room of my own. At bedtime I stretched up and turned off my own light switch and had to find my way to the bed in the dark.

I was alone, and felt lonely. My eyes got used to the dark. A chink of light through the curtains outlined the new location of familiar furniture. I could not sleep, and my tired brain was racing. I hadn't wanted to leave the old house and the snow had prevented me seeing the new neighbourhood. I knew even then I'd never settle in.

I hear unfamiliar voices and footfalls. Sounds carried in a different way to the old house. A click of a pipe might have been the thermostat adjusting and the radiators cooling. And just when I'd got used to it and was dropping off another sound – that seemed exaggeratedly loud – startled me awake. A series of clicks

I imagined to be some giant mouse, its claws clattering over the lino. It was the beams cooling and 'righting' themselves. At dawn the furniture slowly emerged from darkness, asserted itself and laid claim to its new territory.

Not so for Harry. He had no power over the light. For him the sounds that I'd experienced had a different meaning. The creaks were the beams finding a new position, floors below, crammed together like a bonfire or wigwam, not dissimilar in some ways to the trees – over-hanging and entwined – that later were to provide him shelter. The faint, indistinct voices were those of his trapped family. The scratching that of temporarily dislodged mice – a foretaste of the scrubbing for food of squirrels in the wood.

He lay there helpless, his mind blank, not even giving way to the panic conviction of the smell of gas. Nothing had hit him physically. Not outwardly. Waves of sound flooding his ear, from the outer shell to coils and stirrups, threw him off balance. The familiar household flotsam began to engulf him. He tried to swim breast stroke, parting the water in front of him, pushing the debris aside and behind, just looking ahead, for light. And then at the point of drowning all his past comes back to him and is forever locked away.

When the rescuers dig him out, hours or days later, they find a changed person. He does not recognise them, hardly greets them, and doesn't thank them.

And when – to revert to the 'story' – the police next open the cell door they find he has, in 'reliving' the past, forgotten all that has happened since. He can give them no help in their investigations. He is released to begin a new life, which may bear no relation to the life he led in the wood.

Yes. I suppose this could all have been worked up into a story – of novella length.

'Worked up' is probably the right term. Odd – isn't it? – when you have no real substance or facts to go on you always fill the vacuum with apocalyptic imaginings and a snatch of autobiography (inevitably childhood) or a bit of word-play linking disparate chains of thought. Keys unlocking memory. I ask you! Stirrups and being thrown off balance! Balance of the mind! Resonating shell of the ear. What corn! What ears of corn!

No, in trying to make a story of Harry's life I have lost its essence. It went on the same everyday, arrested at a certain stage. Nothing happened to him. That, if anything, was the point. And if anything had happened there would have been no connection between the action and his life, and no more basis for a story than a chance road accident.

Yet his condition still nags in my mind. It resonates and spreads circles, further than the transmission circles around the radio mast.

More than a game of Consequences.

Inconsequences

Inconsequences

Say Hello, Diary, to your new owner.

Did you think you weren't going to get one? I admit twenty-eight days after the beginning of the year is rather long to be waiting on the stationer's shelf.

However, now you've found a purchaser don't expect life to change much. You'll be stuck on the bedside table most of the time. I may forget you for weeks, and then drive you mad with constant attention. You'll get used to my funny little ways.

And please don't expect me to change. We can change – and this is the Thought for the Day – we can change our religion, politics and morals more easily than we can our fingerprint habits.

This, then, Diary, by way of introduction. I have nothing to add. The mere purchase of a diary is an entry momentous enough. Here ends our first official meeting. Pen has touched paper. Consummatum est. You are now my confidante. By continually referring to you I'll learn how I live my life, perhaps even how I should live it. You, much more than I, will divine the drift, swell and undertow.

PS. What I note down is confidential. I'd thought of buying a diary with a clip and lock. But it was expensive and bulky. I wanted something portable that I could refer to at all times.

Feb 18

A three week gap since I last opened you! The first six weeks of the year gone by – without recall – and it was inability to recall that prompted my resolution to keep a diary.

Thought for the Day. What are New Year Resolutions but belated, puritanical reactions to the indulgence of Christmas? Now there's a platitude, if there ever was!

More serious. Failure to record events, however trivial, is to invite the Fates to descend en masse. A diary wards off unexpected and significant events. It's not the great individual happenings that make a diary worth keeping and re-reading. It's the weave of the trivia. Pedestrianism, not being selective, or able to see the wood for the trees, is the hallmark of diary keeping. Even more important is consistent entry. Do this and a pattern will inevitably emerge.

Let's begin on a trivial note. Tonight, on the way home from work, which I can't get away from quickly enough, I waited twenty minutes for a tube! I went to the far end of the platform to avoid the other passengers, but they soon edged to my end. I was about to abandon my wait and walk home when the indicator board claimed a train was due. For once it was correct. I could feel the air rushing along the tunnel.

A child, who'd been making a dreadful noise, quietened down, turned to its mother and said –

'What's that wind, Mummy?'

'It's the train, my love. It's pushing the air down the tunnel in front of it.'

I couldn't resist leaning over and confiding to the nasty little brat.

'It works on the same principle – as a fart.'

I trust, Diary, you are not going to object to mild swear words. I know I'm putting an impress on your paper that can't be totally erased. But I'd rather you didn't try to censure me by fading.

March 13

Another long gap! Are we still talking? Our liaison is not proving mutually successful!

To be honest – and what is a diary for, if not confession? – the reason this diary is empty, is simple. I can barely see my own handwriting. The very proof of the life I am chronicling is lost to me as soon as it is saved, as if what little I do achieve and record is immediately obliterated.

I started wearing contact lenses two years ago – before I moved here or went to my new job. When I first wore them I saw the world afresh, more defined, contained as in a view finder. I could truly claim, 'I see things more clearly than other people'.

I had the world under scrutiny, without the world knowing. I've grown very dependent upon the lenses. I don't regard I'm fully awakened in the morning until I've washed, dressed and, as a finishing touch, put them in. When I take them out at night I fall asleep almost at once. I've never told anyone I wear them. It would be like revealing my thoughts.

Naturally, Diary, I want to share this with you, as a writer would with a reader.

Of course, there are drawbacks. Sometimes the lenses smart if I wear them too long. If I get grit under them I stagger about like a mid-day drunk. If one falls out I freeze, get on my hands and pat the floor in all manner of contortions.

Lately the difficulties have become greater. I've caught a cold, which I can't shake off. I feel run down and have a stye on my eye. The lenses are impossible to wear for more than a couple of hours.

The optician said, 'There's nothing wrong with the lenses. It's your general health.' So I went to the doctor, who said, 'There's nothing wrong with your health. You want to go back to glasses.' (A Moral for the Day somewhere there.) The optician eventually conceded the problem. 'It's not the lenses. It's you. Your eyes are rejecting them.' He advised me to stick to glasses for a month or so.

I was very reluctant. Wearing lenses has been my little secret, my alternative skew on the world. I can't bear the thought of appearing in public in thick glasses. I'd rather stay indoors. But, alas, work precludes this.

And, double alas, it's at work that my vision poses most problems. I can't judge distances and keep bumping into things or tripping – the loose ends of carpets, the electric flexes, the thin legs of tubular-steel chairs. I soon right myself and never blame not having my lenses in. I haven't told the staff I wear them – or rather that I've always worn them – at least since I began this job – but cannot do so at the moment.

Occasionally I misfile something. Or drop a sheaf of papers. How they seem to get the air under them! I never swear. I try to laugh it off by saying –

'These sheets of paper seem to have a life of their own, don't they?' or 'Look, what you've gone and done now, you silly things. I told you to stay there and you disobey me deliberately.' Last week I thought of a new ploy and said – 'I think we've got a resident poltergeist.'

In fact, if anything was knocked over, dropped or misfiled I often said, 'Poltie's been at it again. Can't turn your back without him undoing all the good work you've done.'

I don't think the joke went down well with my colleagues. After the third time I'd said it, I heard one of them whisper – 'The only thing we've got here is a resident poltroon.'

March 14

I came home last night to find one of my windows streaked with an almighty bird dropping. It went the whole length of the window – and as the windows were closed I was at a loss how it could have happened, or what angle the bird was flying. Or, come to that, what type of bird could have done so much. It had obviously eaten an extra helping of blackberries. The whole wretched mess was a pale mauve dotted with purple pips.

It was like some terrible omen, a bolt from the skies. I cleaned it off straightaway – which incidentally wasn't easy because the window cleaning fluid was also a pale mauve colour, and without my lenses it was difficult to tell which was which. I must have applied half the bottle before the window was clean.

I used the rag to wipe the bathroom mirror. This always gets dirty with diluted toothpaste from my vigorous brushing.

I looked at myself close-to. A bit haggard, and the stye on the eye looked very sore. It, too, was a pale mauve colour.

March 16

I often see people in terms of animals. Not people one knows well, but peripheral, negligible people, the sort who pop in and out the office door. They're like minor characters in a novel. If you investigate them too closely you begin to sympathise and lose concentration on the main theme. It's the same with 'real' people. I find by emphasising their similarities to the non-human world, or with fictional characters, I can cope with the contrasts and threats they pose.

Since I've been without my lenses I can't distinguish the staff at work. They are all of a breed and dress similarly. To differentiate them it's necessary to exaggerate their idiosyncrasies and idiocies.

It's the same with names. I've never been good at remembering them. Inventing them, yes. Alliterative mnemonics. Call people by the name of your choice and they don't grow too large in one's consciousness, or stray too much from one's particular definition of them.

They are even more valid if the people really do resemble animals. Mr Boardman, for example, undeniably has a face like a chipmunk, and Mr Sandling looks and dresses like a teddy-bear. And Miss Judith (I never found out her surname) has the features of a fish. She lets her hair flop over her face. Only later do you see the determinedly down-turned mouth and the dead-fish eyes – like a haddock permanently trying to swim through seaweed.

People grow like their names, too. Miss Bowen, from the next office, could only be a Deidre; and Miss Cartlet really is a bit of a Monica. And I always call Edwina Ed-Wee-wee, because she's so drippy.

It's not without its dangers though. Only today, Miss Willings, she of the buck teeth – one never knows if she smiling or snarling, she has a come-hither-ish sneer – asked if I'd seen Mr Boardman.

I replied, 'Oh. Is that the one who looks like a chipmunk?'

I fully expected the reply, 'Yes, I suppose he does a bit, come to think of it. How perceptive of you.'

Instead, I got a frosty, stone-faced response, lips pursed, as far as she was able, which, with her buck teeth, wasn't very far. She gave a dainty heel-click and turned away. And was there perhaps a petulant toss of the head? And a forced resolution in her walk? Did her court shoes clatter on the floor tiles just that little too much? Perhaps I am exaggerating and adding to the story. It happened so quickly and took me so unawares that I cannot remember the exact details.

Personally, I think there's nothing wrong in seeing people as animals. It's my special perception of them. Only on that occasion with Miss Willings have I revealed it to anyone. I shall relish it all the more now I feel obliged to keep it secret.

It's certainly not reprehensible – not, say, in the way that Mr Webb's approach was. He left a few weeks after I arrived. He saw women in terms of flowers. Most offensive he was. To their faces he would call them Rosebud, Petunia, Wallflower, Lotus blossom, but usually just Petal.

'Hello, Petal. Blooming, are we? Blossoming?'

The women shrugged as if he needed humouring or ignoring. He was very persistent. Had events come to a head I would publicly have taken the side of the women. As it was he left the office – to be promoted.

March 19

I still feel down. I'm not sure I'll make work tomorrow. It's Friday, after all. The stye on my eye aches mercilessly. I keep rubbing it with the back of my hand like a dog in pain.

Which actually reminds me of something I forgot to enter. I have to re-read old diary entries to find anything new to write. I remember things on the level of word associations – in this case, dog.

I've been doing exercises to build myself up, nothing too strenuous. I do them in the front room, in a secluded corner that can't be overlooked by the neighbours. One of the exercises is done on all fours. You stretch out an opposite arm and leg as far as you can, then come back to the home position. Repeat with the other arm and leg, and then dip your stomach and arch your back. A bit like a pointer dog freezing, front paw outstretched, back legs poised for flight or pursuit.

As I was pulling, stretching and getting into the rhythm the telephone rang. It's on the far side of the room and rather than stand up – a sudden rise might have made me dizzy – I ran over to it on all fours.

It was a wrong number. The man was very rude, quite churlish, in fact. I cocked up a leg towards the phone and said, 'Piss on you, too,' and slammed down the receiver. I ran back to my corner greatly elated, less perhaps like a dog and more like a baboon swaggering on its knuckles.

March 23

I didn't go to work today either. I had an appointment with the optician.

Even local journeys have their hazards. Without my lenses, I worry about the traffic, and about inadvertently ignoring people. I'm conscious of people looking at me, sometimes staring quite hard. They bare their teeth in what I take to be a rudimentary smile. Or wave to me, perhaps warning me not to step in front of an oncoming vehicle. Any shouting I always assume is directed at me. They must surely know me. For all I know they might be work colleagues on official leave wondering why I'm not at work. I start guiltily and make a mental scramble, fumbling for a name or association. Should I have spotted them and said Hello first? How could I, when I wasn't wearing my lenses? Why worry? Do I really know these people? Do I want to know them? Their eager upturned faces staring at me like pink ovals with dots in them, a pink rabbit blancmange viewed from above.

The optician dropped a bombshell.

'You've developed double vision. It only registers slightly. You may not notice it yourself. It shouldn't get worse. A small percentage of contact-lens wearers get this, especially when they transfer back to glasses.'

'But I haven't – and what is it?'

He explained some technicalities and continued. 'For a time the edges blur, a bit like ghosting on television. Maybe you'll read the same line or paragraph twice, but differently the second time. It is as if two people are reading, jointly approaching the same subject. Almost like sharing your sight with someone else. Disconcerting but nothing to worry about.' He smiled and added, 'The two parts will see eye-to-eye eventually. Give your eyes a rest, time to settle down. No glasses or lenses for a month.'

What a blow! I'd not been conscious of any double vision. But now it's been pointed out I can see what's meant. I certainly do see a bluRRing – or is that a contradiction in terms? How can one see – Thought for the Day – something that is indefinite?

I suppose I often see things in twos - - oCCasionaLLy those pink ovals are just like blancmanges being woBBled so fast that the edges do become bluRRed, just like the uncontroLLably noDDing head of a victim of Parkinson's disease. Or poSSibly there are two heads, suFFiciently synchronised that they lOOk like one!!

April 4

I'm falling foul of MiSS WiLLings. She's getting the wrong impression of me. It was cold at work today and I said Brr! Brr! I rubbed my hands together and stamped my feet. I don't think I overdid it. Brr! Brr! I genuinely do feel the cold.

She looked at me and said, 'What a funny little noise!'

It's not the first time she's reacted like this. Towards the end of one particularly arduous day I yawned and stretched. Well, when you deflate your lungs there is always a temptation, isn't there, to tail off with a wolf-howl? Just as a sneezing fit lends itself to duck-quacking.

I can't see the objection really. After all she goes around making clucking noises to cats and babies.

Of course, I got a sub-zero look. Face set, eyebrows lowered, eyes glinting for a better view.

I suppose sometimes when I cough I do hack a bit. Do I blow my nose too loud? I've never worried about such things before.

Oh, she is fuNNy, is our MiSS WiLLings. She's taken aback by the slightest movement or noise. For a moment she stands her ground then steps back and fluTTers at the edges. She wears long, lOOse clothing and floPPy collars and baGGy sleeves. All duNN-coloured with floral paTTerns; all gathered and biBBed, with no expanse of taut material. I'm not sure what shape she is underneath. There's something diminutive about her. She reminds me of a hedge-sparrow – shy, nervous, in the shade, close to the hedgerow. Always twiTTering, fluTTering, bEE-busy.

The country name for hedge sparrow is dunnock.

From now on, MiSS WiLLings, you are – the DuNNock.

(Perhaps there's a bit of wagtail in her as well!)

April 12

Another long wait for the tube tonight. Just as the train came in – I'd been waiting for ten minutes – a couple, giggly and clutching each other – ran onto the platform and gasped, 'Isn't that good? Didn't we do well? How convenient! It couldn't've been timed better. Just for US!'

They obviously didn't appreciate how long I'd been waiting, still less that I should have prior claim to a seat. They tried to push past to the only two adjacent seats. But I got there first. They had to sit apart. I tried to look at their expressions – not directly, of course, but as reflected in the windows and glaSS paneLLing. I couldn't quite get them in focus.

There was a large spider in the bath tonight. I was not sure what it was at first. It looked like a cracked egg-shell or a shattered eye. Harmless enough, and in no way an invader of my territory. On the other hand if I can't see things properly I expect them to let me know of their presence by making extra noise. I flushed it down the plughole, which was presumably where it came from.

April 13

At tea-breaks we're all supposed to come together, liaise and socialise, oil the machinery, let the barriers fall, and bask equally in the radiance of the tea-urn.

I find it such an effort. Miss Judith was compiling her shopping list, thinking aloud, name-dropping the expensive exotica she secretly hoped we'd ask her about. She was biting the end of a pencil – like that woman on the Ptolomaic coffin cover – trying to look profound and thoughtful about such concepts as cheese straws and custard tarts. Every so often she muttered the domestic equivalent of Eureka – 'Yes, of course, mustn't forget the ...'

As she scribbled and nibbled in her funny little hen-like way I turned to her and smiled indulgently. 'You won't forget your eggie-peggies, will you?'

She immediately tautened and said in an icy voice, 'I suppose you mean eggs?'

Well, of course, I did, as she well knew.

Lord, how she glowered! She stood up on her hind legs and swayed slightly, making a clucking noise like a blackbird that's just seen a cat.

Huh! She's not averse to joke words when it suits her. Only last week Mr Sandling, who I'm sure has a crush on her, was pouring out the tea, and as he held out a spoon laden with sugar, he said to her, 'Shug? Shug?' She smiled back without replying, as much as to say, 'You know I'm sweet enough already.'

I think he knew how many sugars she took. I've long suspected something between them. Well, he's welcome to her.

But why is it I'm snapped at? And for the very same thing that makes her think Mr Sandling is Lord Pink of Perfection!

Trouble again when I got home tonight. No refuge anywhere.

I keep rubbing my eyes with the back of my hands. I'm sure I have hay fever, though it's the wrong time of the year.

My hearing's become more acute. I can hear telegraph wires and car aerials, the whirr of meters, light bulbs, a radio that's on standby. I can anticipate doorbells and phones before they ring. I find continuous noises, the buzzing and droning of office machinery and suchlike, very annoying. The more so if they're not quite distinct.

There's a lot of whispering at work I can't make out. I'm sure it never went on when I had my lenses. But there it is, the minute I come into the office. Sometimes I think I hear my name.

Tonight at home I was plagued by a fly. It sounded like an alarm clock gone shrill with speeding-up. I was reading in the front room when I heard the buzzing in the hallway. I opened the door – just the minimum – but enough alas for the fly to slip in. I couldn't see it, but I knew the general direction it was flying, and tried to swat it with my book.

Large Print Books are such a boon, aren't they? Bold print and dark ink! Even if the range of titles is only fit for old ladies.

Yet despite the print size I still get double vision. I trace my index finger under each line I read. This is a prompt for concentration – an asset in this case, as the book is tedious. The police are trying to identify the body of a woman. They think she was a prostitute and have called her Madame X.

As I poised my finger over a line the X of Madame X seemed to come alive and move by itself. Was I seeing double? Had the X acquired little legs? Was it the fly? Were the transparent wings giving a blurred outline to the letter? It moved from left to right along the print, then it jumped down a line – like the cursor on a word processor. When it came to the next mention of Madame X it stopped right on the top of the X – and just before a question mark.

I snapped the book shut, hoping to hear a rewarding crunch. But there was nothing. I didn't bother to re-open it. I'd lost the page. It all hardly matters. I don't care who killed Madame X. Wasn't me.

April 18

Looking back on last week's diary entry – I always read the previous few entries before writing a new one – I am reminded of one of my greatest triumphs in separating couples.

I'd gone out for a meal straight from work to give myself one of those treats I no longer concern myself with. It was early evening and the restaurant was empty. I took a table in the corner, a table for four. It was raised up a few steps and offered a splendid vantage. I was in no hurry – which was as well for the items I'd chosen seemed to take the longest to prepare. By the time I got the first course most of the tables had been filled.

No sooner had I finished the appetiser than a family unit of four walked in and looked round for an empty table. They glowered at me as much as to say 'Why is that person sitting there ALONE on that table for four? We should get priority over single people. Anyone else would have realised we were a family, the basic unit of society, happy and united, and made way for us accordingly.'

I was surprised they didn't complain to the waiter or ask me to move to another table. I looked sour, scraped my plate and put an imaginary forkful to my lips in case they thought I'd finished.

After further discussion and significant looks at their watches they decided to stay. The children seemed tired and hungry. They split up; mother and son on one table; father and daughter on a not quite adjacent table. It didn't take long for the situation to deteriorate. They went back and forth explaining to each other what they thought the menu items were. The mother tried to control the child at the father's table, and the father the child at the mother's table.

'Amanda says she wants plaice.'

'Amanda doesn't like plaice. You should know that by now. She is your daughter.'

'Well, she says she wants it and she's the one who'll be eating it.'

'She can't have it. It would be a waste of money.'

'I'll be paying for it. We did come to give her a treat. It is her birthday.'

'That's nothing to do with it.'

'But Mummy, I want plaice.'

'Well, you can't have it. It's got too many bones.'

'Boo hoo! Boo hoo!'

I laughed to myself. All the other customers glowered at them. The waiters hated them. Single people, couples, or foursomes are the waiter's ideal. The occasional staff party is tolerated, but families with children never.

The waiter's attitude warmed towards me, as if saying, 'You stay there, sir. Don't let them have their way. I've seen their sort before. They've shown themselves in their true colours. We were taken in by them at first, but now we see you were right, sir. We keep replacing the knives they drop on the floor. It's not our fault if bloody little Roy gets served before sodding little Amanda. And I bet there'll be a query with the bill. And a mess on the tablecloth. And no bloody tip. Stick to your guns, sir. More coffee? A pleasure. On the house.'

I felt expansive, substantial and deep-rooted. I'd stage-managed the whole entertainment, set a trap, pulled the strings and won the audience over to my side.

April 19

I'm not sure I should have made yesterday's entry. It shows me in a bad light. I have this theory that a diary should sometimes be left to mature, ferment and fuse. When re-opened the taste will be different, and give some indication of those threads that have a worthwhile future.

Whenever I read former entries – and I can barely read my handwriting, my eyesight having made me write badly in the first place thus making the deciphering doubly difficult – I am amazed at what seemed important then; the little daily syphonings-off of spleen, the trivial items I invested with significance and recorded at length for safekeeping or to exorcise from memory. The passage of time lends preposterousness to our former strong feelings.

April 20

Diary, I must apologise. You are getting less sleep than I am.

I was awakened this morning about 2.30 by a scraping noise, followed by a hopping as if something was dropping onto the carpet at regular intervals. At first I thought it was a frog, but when it progressed off the edge of the carpet the noise changed to a clattering – as of sharp nails on wood. Or a scratching of a pen on parchment.

I lay still in the dark, my eyes adjusting, testing themselves against a shaft of street light through a chink in the curtains. I listened intently, the blood pumping behind my ears. I felt a draught from under the skirting boards, as if they weren't flush with the wall and a hollow passage existed behind. There were clicks and scurries which might have been the radiators cooling down or the beams righting themselves. A strange popping noise resembled insect eggs hatching or air pressure rustling ear drums. I creaked the bed, drummed my feet and turned on the light.

Mice can get anywhere, through any crevice. They are like thieves. If they're determined to get in they will, whatever you do to prevent them. Once you have them they spread, and then the rats move in.

I couldn't see or do anything, and decided to make a pot of tea. I slipped on my shoes, rather than my slippers, which could be bitten through, and tiptoed into the kitchen. My hand was shaking so much while I was spooning the tea-leaves into the pot that some leaves fell onto an already dirty draining board. I cleaned them off with a kitchen towel and noticed a couple of leaves had smudged. They weren't leaves at all, but mouse droppings. Here was positive confirmation. There are – Thought for the Day – no droppings without life. And sadly, vice versa.

I made a fresh pot of tea and sat in the front room, feeling vulnerable. I'd once read of a mouse that had run down a sleeping man's throat and into his stomach where it frantically clawed his innards causing a fatal haemorrhage. Personally if that had happened to me I would've drunk gallons of water and drowned the bloody thing. But that's as may be.

When I finally did return to bed I folded the counterpane to the centre so as to leave nothing trailing. I left the light on, and filled in this diary.

April 21

This morning I got to work late. Someone – I'm not sure who – said, 'We thought you were going to take the whole day off – again.'

I ignored the comment. The problem of the mouse was uppermost in my mind. In daylight and away from the scene of the incident I felt more collected. I knew I must take decisive action. I thought of some of the things dynamic Mr Boardman often says.

"We've got to take positive action. Unpleasant decisions have to be made. We cannot let things slide. We must make a stand and confront the problem without fudging. I have explained the situation. I have limited sympathy."

Well, he never had much sympathy for anything. What else was it he said?

"There is no alternative. I am being forced into action I would prefer not to have to take. I do not consider the fault is mine."

It never was with him! How was it he always went on?

"Managerial decisions haff-to-be-taken."

And what came after that?

"Decisions of State haff-to-be taken. It is our duty now to push through with them."

Hitherto I'd thought talk like this was just so much garbage. Whenever I'd been on the receiving end I'd laughed in his face. Was he right after all? At least in certain circumstances? Dealing with the mouse being one of them? Mr Boardman, I'm sure, would have appreciated this.

So, I asked to leave early in the evening as I had something of great importance to do. I was told – with a marked lack of understanding – 'I thought you were going to make up for being late.' I asked to see Mr Boardman, who I knew would be more understanding, now I'd begun to share his way of seeing things. Unfortunately he was out. I left without further ado.

On the way home I made the crucial decision and bought a mousetrap. Then I mellowed. The mouse was an unwitting dumb animal, to be ensnared for being itself. It merely wanted to live and eat. I knew that it couldn't go on living where it was, but at least it could eat a good meal before it died. It was nothing personal and to make that plain I popped into the delicatessen for some cheese.

Which cheese would it prefer? Cheddar would be too common, almost an insult. Soft cheese wouldn't fit into the trap. Blue vein cheese might be a little strong. Gouda and Edam too rubbery. How about Emmenthal? I've always called it Episcopal Cheese because it's full of holes – and therefore Holy. I'm sure the mouse would appreciate the holes! Ha! Ha! Whenever I bought it – which wasn't often – I used it sparingly. I was fond of nibbling the edges. It's especially good for that. You can see your tooth marks and however lightly you nibble the cheese turns pale where it's been bitten. I bought a fair-sized portion, so I could have some for myself. The mouse and I will eat the same food just to show there's no ill-will.

I opened the front door gingerly and looked round saying, or rather quoting – Quote of the Day,

"Nibble, nibble Mousekin
Who's nibbling at my Housekin?"

I set the trap. I've never set a trap for anything or anybody before. Who knows that one mightn't be being set for me?

'It's hard cheese for you, mousey-wousey. Holey cheese. Your favourite.'

I put the trap on the kitchen floor and had a cheese salad myself. It was a waiting game from now on. All evening I sat in the front room expecting to hear the trap snap shut. But it is still intact as I write this.

Two days running, Diary, and I've had to fill you in twice. At night and in the morning. Everything is in twos these days. I'm not sure how to date this double entry, yesterday's or today's.

About 3am it was. I'd left the bedroom door open. I heard a sound like a gunshot, followed by the deepest silence.

I delayed going into the kitchen. The mouse deserved a few moments' grace. I wanted it fully dead before I went out. I wasn't up to giving the coup de grace.

The trap had snapped and recoiled across the floor. The cheese had gone, but there was no dead mouse.

'We have a clever little mouse here. It won't prove a match for me. There will be further action. I must harden my heart.'

I was late again for work – whichever day it is. I really can't worry about time-keeping. There was only one thing on my mind and I didn't want anything at the office to intrude.

The office is located near a hospital. The windows were open and the noise of the ambulances coming and going became quite unbearable. To diffuse my irritation I chanced a little pleasantry with MiSS WiLLings.

'They seem to be getting closer all the time, don't they?'

She stared at me for a moment.

'The ambulances I mean.'

'Oh, yes,' she smiled – or rather bared her buck teeth. 'They'll soon be coming to take you away.'

Well, honestly. I don't know what prompted her to say that. If she knew my troubles she'd have thought twice. What a comment! Why me? It would have been more appropriate for one of her former admirers. Mr Clissold, for instance. Every time an ambulance went by HE used to go Er-ar! Er-ar! Er-ar!

At least things are pleasanter at home. Whenever I go into the kitchen now I make a little squeaking noise, laughing to myself, 'Pussy'll come and get you.'

I wanted to see my adversary so after setting the trap – and nibbling a bit of cheese myself – I crouched under the table, motionless and silent. On several occasions I thought I saw something flash out the corner of my eye. But it might only have been an early symptom of a stroke or brain tumour.

As I nibbled the cheese I almost wished it were friable, and I had to scurry for broken bits, clean my whiskers and preen myself. You can cup your wrists as well as your palms to get the effect. I haven't mastered the noise yet and resort to a feeble EEK! EEK! I often clatter my nails on empty biscuit tins.

What it is to be so small! Living in someone else's house, unable to take in the hugeness of the surroundings, more responsive to noise than sight, forever peeping out from a secure hideaway. Timid, too. Oh, I know the feeling. And preferring night to day. I can understand that, as well. Walking in the shadows, keeping close to walls and hedges, snuggling in secluded corners.

And yet, mouse, you must die. As we all must. And be trapped, not knowing why.

After several hours under that table, I got stiff and bored and went to bed.

April 22

I was late again this morning. More remarks were made.

'When transport is bad one leaves home earlier.'

'As far as I know,' I said, unforthcomingly, 'transport is OK.' I was not going to tell them about the mouse.

MiSS WiLLings spent much of the day looking in my direction. At four o'clock she came over and said that I'd been staring into space for over an hour.

'Standing there,' she said. 'Just like a heron.'

A comparison I deeply resented. A heron! I must admit I have never thought of MYSELF in terms of an animal!

I suppose it was her way of getting back at me for saying that Mr Boardman looked like a chipmunk. No doubt she'd run off and told him.

I've used up all the cheese now. I had a good nibble myself. It's that sort of cheese, isn't it? I must admit though that I prefer something more substantial to bite and tear at.

Do you remember those splendid slabs of nougat, encrusted with nuts and cherries? Other confectionery may rot your teeth but these positively strengthen them. You bite at the slabs, leave tooth marks in them, tear at them. The slab twists and contorts itself and is very difficult to break. And when you manage to separate a piece – and you have little control over the size of the piece twisted off – then it's sheer murder to chew. Your jaws ache for days.

Well, I'm not sure what prompted me to do it – my little Joke of the Day, I suppose. I'd been going to that tobacconist's for years – a model customer. On this occasion after the usual, 'Good evening, how are you?' I pointed to the slabs of nougat and said,

'Nitty Nutty Nougat
One Two Three
Diddle-Iddle-Aye-Doe
He! He! He!

The tobacconist looked at me without expression. He must have pushed a security bell hidden behind the counter. His son, whom I'd seen grow up from a boy, emerged from the back of the shop and pushed me into the street.

All those years of feigned personal service! Oh, the dentured smiles of the short-weight-givers!

April 24

Nothing on the work front today, thank goodness. Or at least nothing that concerned me. MiSS WiLLings and the others spent at least half an hour this morning huddled in a charmed circle, like gibbering gibbons frightened by a leopard. Miss Judith seemed to be enumerating telling points on her fingers. Or possibly, she might have been trying to pull off a pink rubber glove. I couldn't quite see.

On the walk home from the station I was conscious of being followed – by clicking heels. They crossed whenever I crossed, but they never caught up. I couldn't shake them off. I've always found this annoying. I would rather people felt I was following them.

However, I forgot them when I saw a cat sitting on the wall outside the flats. At first I thought it was a large rat. Once mice move in, rats always follow. It was perched unconcerned, even though the wall's embedded with glass, and sunning itself, its front paws tucked under its chest, folded away to its minimum size and solidarity; the pose a sculptor would find easiest, with no limbs or tail to break off. It stood up slowly, blinked, stretched nonchalantly and jerked up its tail.

'Come to catch the mouse, have you? Been sent? By Providence?'

I snapped my fingers, clucked and made a kissing noise. The cat immediately dropped off the far side of the ledge. The footsteps behind me hurried past. The person – a young woman – appeared to think I was making the clucking noise at her. She flatters herself, clicking her court shoes at an angle of ten-to-two! Like DoBBin on the CoBBles!

Diary, it's good to be able to turn to you. Just a quick entry. I know it's all out of sequence. I filled in yesterday's entry on time – and today's will, God willing, be done later. But where does one put things that happen in the middle of the night, that is past midnight? The end of yesterday's entry, or the beginning of today's? It's the old question. I've tended to put anything to do with the mouse in the following day's entry as the presence of the mouse posed problems that would have to be dealt with in the future. But what of dreams? They relate to what has gone on in the past. I've decided to enter dreams as a rider or postscript to the day's events. Though, as nothing much happened today there should really have been no dream.

(All this would not be so much of a problem if I weren't waking up so much.)

The dream I had last night – no tonight (I am writing this the following morning, though dating it yesterday) – concerned MiSS WiLLings. She appeared more than once. I can't recall the circumstances of the first. The second time she spoke. These days without my lenses – not that they should affect dreams – I remember speech rather than sight.

She asked, 'Do you recognise me?'

'Yes, but you look different.'

'Yes,' she said. 'I've had my buck teeth removed.'

'It makes your lips look fuller.'

'That's why I had them removed. I did it for you.' She paused. 'Do you like it?'

I paused. 'Did it cost much?'

'Yes,' she replied. 'But there's plenty left over for us to have a good time together.'

That was the first section of the dream. I must have half-woken – and lost the thread. When I dropped off again MiSS WiLLings reappeared, this time with her buck teeth back in place. She bared them continually in a provocative display.

'I've been keeping an eye on you,' she said. 'Most of the time you seem to be doing nothing. But I know that in reality there are momentous things going on in your mind. Yes, I've been watching you for some time. As you must know.'

I did not reply.

'I sensed you were different when I first saw you. Little signs that indicated your true nature. For example, those little mistakes you make in typing. Some may think they were mere inefficiency, incompetence, wilfulness even. But not I! I have watched you at the keyboard, your hands poised like a pianist waiting for the cue from the conductor. And then enraptured you have typed – what to others might seem mere gobbledygook, a continuous, un-spaced fusion of letters, numbers and punctuation marks – but which to me is something of deep portent. Randomness is impossible with the Inspired. There is a pattern in seeming chaos, a profound significance. But not only this,' she continued, 'your little snatches of song, the funny little phrases, the odd endings to words – these are not mere word play or jokey gibberish. They are part of something altogether grander. The very Gift of Tongues. The mystic language, age-old … and …'

The scene changed to a concert hall with rows of impassive faces looking in my direction as I sat at the keyboard about to play a piano transcription of an orchestral masterpiece, my memory so good I needed no score or musical prompt, and my finger span grown unnaturally large to encompass all the instruments, from bass-drum tremolo to the gilt-edging of piccolo.

But the music that came out was a clatter, all at the same pitch, with the occasional warning bleep, followed by the machine rattle of the printer.

I sought refuge under the piano lid, my uncontrollably twitching feet aiming to dislodge the prop, my hands gathering at the triplicate wires, making great harp swoops, not deadened by a placating hand.

Then mercifully, I must have rolled over onto an exposed spring in the mattress. I was conscious of something prodding me to wake up. Which I did, shouting accusingly at the audience, 'You could have left! You could have left! I never expected clapping.'

I lay there, aware my work life had trespassed into my sleeping hours, much more of an intrusion than a fly or mouse. My privacy had been invaded with the aim of telling me how I was regarded at work. I resolved to change my image.

That, then, is yesterday's entry completed today. In fact filling in this entry now – one must write dreams down quickly or they are gone – has probably made me late for work – which was something I wanted to avoid.

Yes. Yes. I was late. On the very day I wanted to create a good impression. If you leave home a quarter of an hour late you can be sure that it will be compounded so that you arrive at work one hour and a quarter late.

The journey was depressing. The tubes were out of action. Nothing seemed to be going my way – neither the buses nor the course of my personal history. When I caught a bus it stuck in a traffic jam.

I sat impatient, eager and tensed for a day of making good. I devised a prayer that I knew would be fulfilled. It is – God, have I come to this? – The Prayer of the Day.

I transcribe it direct from my note-book before progressing to the main events of the day. It is called the Prayer of the Public Places.

Please let the people walking in front of me suddenly stop dead so I bump into them.

Please step out of a doorway in front of me.

Please don't look when you are turning a corner.

Please ram your push-chair or shopping trolley into my ankles.

Please poke the spokes of your umbrella into my eye.

Please let me get caught up in a school outing or a guided tour.

Please do not form a queue at the bus stop.

Please let the innocent school children and frail old ladies push in front of me.

Please do not signal when your car is turning the corner.

Please jump the traffic lights so I am made to run to the half-way bollard like a frightened hare.

And PLEASE do not speak clearly when you shout out from your car window – in case I am able to distinguish apology from abuse.

Please let the pavement be irregular and when it is raining let me tread on a stone that sinks down and fills my shoes with water.

Above all, please let there be a squidge of dog shit under the particular leaf that for some reason I want to crush underfoot.

When I got to work – hopelessly late – no adverse comments were made. In fact, everyone seemed to be extra nice. Mr Boardman mercifully was at some hastily convened meeting.

I was determined to make a good impression. Wearing my lenses was the only way. I knew they'd be painful at first. I could not possibly wear them for a whole day so I economised. After the morning tea break I went to the loo and put them in. They were very sore. My face puckered in discomfort. I sat it out and remained at my desk about half an hour, reaffirming distances and positions, getting the exact delineation of edges and trying to eradicate the effects of the double vision.

I kept looking at Miss Willings. I screwed up my eyes to see clearly. I winced a smile of pain and she, on the other side of the desk, half-smiled and grimaced through her buck-teeth. I have an awful feeling that she and Miss Judith (whose surname I never knew) are one and the same. The floppy hair, plus the teeth, plus the droopy dresses.

Oh God! Almost every day I have crossed swords with one or the other. I have even tried to play them off against each other. And they are the same! How victimised she must think herself. I must prove myself by working hard.

I set out in earnest, walking confidently and quickly from one part of the office to the other. At one stage I got a bit of grit under the lens and staggered about like a drunk. But it soon blinked itself clear. The office reaction was minimal.

I completed the first batch of work, and went to fetch more. As I was carrying the heavy bundle of papers I felt that dread sensation that anyone who's ever worn lenses can appreciate. It's like being hit in the eye, going from light to shade, being suddenly presented with a change of scene, or looking at a film when the projector fails. One of the lenses had popped out, rejected like a transplanted organ. I froze in mid-track – and uttered a colossal expletive.

I held the papers awkwardly in one arm and patted my face and clothes in the hope that the lens would drop down. Nothing did. It was obviously on the floor already. I dared not move for fear of treading on it. I wasn't quite near enough a desk to put the papers down. So I threw them. It happened to be onto Mr Boardman's desk. He hates anything being put on his desk. It's always clear. He's always up-to-date in his work. The wadge of papers slid along the surface – which was the most highly polished in the office – dislodged the pen-holder and knocked the phone off the hook. This – combined with my expletive – caused considerable consternation among the staff.

But I could not heed their objections and merely said, 'Please be quiet. Something has happened.'

I knelt on my heels, balancing myself on the outstretched fingers of one hand. I knew I had to be consistent and divide the floor into imaginary sections, checking each thoroughly. It is actually easier to do this if the floor has some sort of pattern. This one was plain. I mapped out a circle about four feet around me and moved carefully in the centre investigating each segment. It was awkward looking around with one lens in and one lens out. I screwed up the dud eye and tilted my head and held it near the floor, like a thrush listening for a worm, but really hoping that some glint of light would catch the lens. It was not particularly sunny. I glanced up to see the staff, looking down at me, muttering among themselves.

I feared the windows might be open, and the lens would be dislodged by the breeze. I shouted. 'Willings, Judith, close the windows, will you!' Seemingly they were closed anyway.

I gently patted the floor. Lenses do tend to travel – and, like mice, they can get into corners, crevices and the smallest chink. They defy gravity. They have the ability to disappear – not merely to be transparent but actually to vanish. I called out to it.

'Where are you? You do have a life of your own, don't you? Why are you trying to escape? Don't you know your master? Don't you want to be re-inserted?'

I manoeuvred myself round to study another segment. The staff seemed to be closing in, muttering inane comments such as 'water divining'. I shouted to them, 'Go away. You must not get closer. You must not tread within the Circle.'

They moved back. My knees and ankles were now beginning to ache and I readjusted myself, trying to make the minimum of body contact with the floor. I was helped in this by the exercises I used to do in the corner of my front room. In fact to relax myself I did a few of the exercises there and then – especially the one on all fours where you hollow and arch your lower back and thrust your abdomen forward. I was quite near the table by now and took the opportunity of crawling under it. I scanned the floor for the offending lens. Then took a breather. When I got up I banged my head, dislodged the phone, caused a drawer to half open and, of course, I shouted another expletive.

In the open drawer were Mr Boardman's cigarettes and box of matches. I leaned over, grabbed the matches, struck one and held it in front of me like a brand. I cried out,

'Oh. Element. Glint and reflect on the Glass Concavity.'

I had to use four or five matches before I found the lens. It was right in the middle of where I'd already searched. I was so scared that I might drop it again that I lay on my back and inserted it from above. I blinked, tested my eye, rubbed it with the back of my wrist and laughed out loud.

'Thank God. I am Whole again.'

I could not resist a little dance on the place the lens had fallen. Then I strode purposefully to the door – through the glass panel of which the staff had been peering. I yanked it open and cried,

'I am Whole again. Rejoice. You may enter. Come. Do.'

Two of them ventured in and walked over to Mr Boardman's desk.

'Oh, leave that,' I said efficiently. 'I'll tidy it up.'

Then Mr Boardman himself came in. His meeting must have ended early. Miss Willings was with him and gasped, 'Look the matches are still on the floor. Your matches. There's four, no five of them.'

I don't know what she was going on about and I don't think Mr Boardman did either because he ignored her and smiled at me, called me aside and said casually, 'Do you want to have the afternoon off? You're very welcome.'

I looked at him in surprise.

'You've got through a lot of work today.'

This was true. And it was good to have the fact acknowledged. I'd been determined to make a concerted effort. This had obviously been noted and even transmitted to people not actually in the office. This was very gratifying. Perhaps he had subconsciously known I looked to him when dealing with the mouse problem. So, despite a bad start I felt I had made out well.

It was odd going home early. There weren't the usual crowds. Mercifully Dobbin on the Cobbles did not follow me. The cat, however, was there again, on the wall beside the flats.

'So, you've come to see me again, have you, Puss? Can't keep away. Eager to get the mouse?'

I was grateful it had waited outside, and not barged in uninvited like the other infestations. I've always had this way with animals, an instinctive attraction. I prefer them to humans. You can wean them on food and they will come back. Cupboard love perhaps, but I can cope with that. In future incarnations I'd like to be an animal, though I'm not yet sure which one.

I stretched up to the cat and rubbed my fingers against its silky fur. It meowed and jerked up its tail.

'Well, do you want to come in? I've got a nice mouse for you to catch. At least I think I have.'

It turned elegantly on its paw pads and swished its tail uncertainly. It stopped as if interested in some movement or sound, a rustle in the hedge or someone passing in the distance. I looked in the same direction. Perhaps like me it mistook curled leaves for mice. Nonetheless I was peeved it was not giving me its full attention.

'You don't want to come in then? Playing hard to get, are you? You're only a stray. Can you afford to be so choosy and ignore my attentions? Would you like to catch a mousey-wousey? You shall have nice times. You shall go to the ball, Pussinda Belinda.'

It showed no inclination to move.

'Oh, come on, Pussy. Think of that mouse. Wouldn't you like to play with it?'

It jerked up its tail.

'Yes, I thought you'd like that. You'll lose interest when it stops twitching, won't you? Come free me of the plague of mice. Pretend I'm a mouse.'

It looked away.

'What, lose interest in me, would you? But I'm the reason you came here, aren't I? No? Then take that.'

I pushed it over the wall.

Looking back that was the longest diary entry I ever made.

I'm not sure what came over me! I don't know what it is exactly I'm supposed to have done that's so reprehensible.

Seemingly after I'd pushed the cat over the wall I turned round and shouted. 'It wouldn't play. It was rude to me. It broke its promise. It's not hurt. It's not dead. Can't you see? There's no glass the other side. It's not shattered. It still glints and reflects, and at a certain angle obscures what's underneath.'

They all listened in stony silence in that room, didn't they? Were there two rows of people listening – or given my double vision – just one? A jury of twelve or a half dozen student doctors? They all looked the same.

The man in charge, though, was different. He had the same pink blancmange features, but on top he had long white hair. He was the Wise Man.

And these people who keep visiting me! I'd almost rather they were in uniforms or white coats. It would at least make it official. I hate the one who looks like a mandrill. And even more the one who visits me every day, with a beard and no moustache. He looks like a Boer. He comes to constrict me. He is a boar, a boor and a bore.

I told him I see far more clearly than most people but without my lenses I have double vision. I've had to share my whole outlook on the world. I cannot be sure if I have seen something, or how many somethings there were. And when I speak an imaginary listener takes over what I am saying.

I asked for my lenses back but I haven't been given them. One of the men doubted I ever wore them.

I almost said, 'And when I re-read a diary entry it is almost as if an imaginary reader finds the thread and continues it.'

No, I never mentioned you, Diary. If they could take you away from me, they would. They'd use you against me.

Snap shut, there's no more to record. You should've had a metal clasp and lock, so I could lose the key.